VAMPIRE ADDICTION:

The Vampires of Athens, Book One

Eva Pohler

Published by Green Press

VAMPIRE ADDICTION: THE VAMPIRES OF ATHENS, BOOK ONE. . Copyright 2015 by Eva Pohler.

FIRST EDITION

Book Cover Design by Benjaminoftomes at Crisp Quartz Design

Library of Congress Cataloging-in-Publication has been applied for

ISBN – 978-0-9862214-1-5

TABLE OF CONTENTS

Chapter One: The Boy on the Bus

"I hadn't realized you packed *that* coat," Gertie's mother complained as Gertie and her parents were leaving their room at the Hotel Excelsior in Venice. "It's not one of your best."

It was a gray puffer coat that tied at the waist and had a soft flannel lining.

"Then it's a good thing you won't have to look at it," Gertie muttered.

Her father glared at her but didn't comment. Instead, he went ahead of her through the lobby to the front desk to check out.

On the way to the ferry, in the back of the limo, Gertie sat across from her parents and said, "It's still not too late to change your minds."

"We're not having this discussion again," her father said. "End of story."

"Don't worry, Gertrude. You'll have the time of your life."

Somehow, Gertie doubted that.

"I know *I* did," her mother added. "I'm jealous of you, actually."

Gertie frowned. "You're welcome to go in my place."

Her mother leaned forward and patted Gertie's knee. "Everyone's frightened of trying new things."

1

She flinched, unused to being touched. "I'm not," she lied. "I just like my own bed."

"It will be there for you when you get back," her father said. "You're seventeen, now. It's time for you to venture away from the nest."

"Happy Birthday to me," she muttered beneath her breath.

Gertie tried to ignore the fact that they were more excited for her to go than she was. She'd never heard of two people more eager to become empty-nesters than her parents. And it wasn't like she was the last in a long line of siblings. She was an only child—an independent one at that. Why couldn't she stay in her room and be left alone?

She wasn't surprised when they didn't get out of the limo and walk her to the ferry. Instead, they had their driver do it. They had offered plenty of excuses—it was too windy out for her mother's asthma and too sunny for her fair skin. Plus her father had a heart condition. And so on and so forth.

Once she was onboard and inside her cabin, she sat on the bed and cried. She hated her parents for making her do this. They had told her to enjoy the scenic boat ride along the Adriatic Sea, but she was determined to spend it all indoors. She rummaged through her bag, found her e-reader, and read until she fell asleep.

It was dark the next day when she got off the ferry in Patras to board the bus to Athens. So much for seeing the sights.

The wind blew strands of her blond hair into her mouth, her eyes, and the sweaty crease of her neck. It wasn't cold—was actually quite warm—but she was glad to have her coat as she pulled her bags behind her.

Gertie expected more people to be riding the bus, but there were only three: an older couple sitting together in the front seat and a boy her age near the back. He was cute and was looking at her with interest. She sat two seats in front of him, without returning his gaze.

"People like you don't usually ride the bus at night," he said after a few minutes. His Greek accent was thick and sexy.

She glanced back at him. "People like me?"

"Young and wealthy."

"Well, if you want to rob me, go for it."

He laughed. "I don't want to rob you."

"The bus driver seems to think so," she said. "He keeps looking at us in his mirror."

"He's bored and has nothing else to do."

She didn't reply, but pulled out her phone and logged on to Goodreads.

"You must be pretty hot," he said after a while.

"I beg your pardon?" She felt a blush coming on.

"In that coat. It's eighty degrees."

"Yeah. I didn't have room in my luggage." She spoke without turning back to face him, while scrolling through

Goodreads on her phone. She wanted to update her status on where she was in her book.

"Where are you going?" he asked.

"Athens."

"I guessed that much. Are you going to visit relatives?"

"Nope."

"Then you must be one of those visiting students," he said, moving to the seat behind hers.

He smelled like soap.

"Yep. You nailed it."

"I did what?"

"I'm sorry. That's just an expression." She glanced back at him. His face was so close, that she could see the big round pupils in his dark brown eyes. His dark curly hair fell around his face, nearly touching his shoulders, which were bare except for the one-inch strap of his blue cotton tank. The muscles in his arms were solid and well defined. If he weren't so cute, she might be uncomfortable.

When she looked into his eyes, she found it difficult to pull away. He was mesmerizing.

Her phone vibrated, stirring her from her stupor. It was a text from her mother, asking if she had landed yet in Patras.

"On bus to Athens," she texted back.

When the boy said nothing more, she rummaged through her bag for her e-reader and returned to the world of her book.

Not thirty minutes had passed when she felt the boy lean on the back of her seat and ask, "What are you reading?"

"*Interview with the Vampire*, by Anne Rice."

He gasped.

She spun around to face him. "Have you read it?"

"No, no. Is it good?"

"So far, yes. I'm loving it." Then she added, "I've always been fascinated by vampire stories."

The corners of his mouth quirked. "Is that so?"

"What's so funny?" She narrowed her eyes. "I don't believe in them or anything; I'm just interested in the mythology."

"I see."

She didn't like that he was laughing at her, so she turned around in her seat to face the front and continued reading. It was difficult for her to get back into the novel after that. She kept seeing the boy's face in place of the words.

Only a few minutes had passed, however, when the boy leaned forward and asked, "So what interests you? About the vampires?"

"A lot of things." She glanced back at him. "Their superpowers, for one: invisibility, flight, mind control..."

"Don't forget x-ray vision," he said, giving her a once over.

"Yeah. Right." She laughed. "You're thinking of Superman."

He laughed, too. "What else?"

She turned in her seat and rested her back against the bus window so she could face him. "I guess the idea of conquering death is interesting to me."

"Are you afraid of death?"

"No. Not really. But I suppose I'm curious about it."

"In what way?" He leaned closer.

"Well, don't you wonder if there's life after death? Do we go to heaven? Or do we go to sleep? Or do we just stop existing? Not that it matters. I just wonder, that's all."

"If it doesn't matter, then why do you wonder about it?"

"It *matters*. I just meant we're going to die regardless of what happens." She twisted the belt of her coat. "Like my grandma. She just died. And so I wonder if she can still hear me and stuff, you know?"

He sat back in his seat and studied her, like he was assessing her.

She blushed. "What?"

He shook his head. "So what else about vampire *mythology* do you find interesting?"

"I don't know." She twisted the belt in the opposite direction. "The combination of power and powerlessness, I guess. It makes them tragic."

"Powerlessness?"

"They can't help what they are. They don't usually choose to become vampires."

"But they prey on humans, yes?" he asked.

"In the story I'm reading right now, a vampire is trying to live on the blood of animals, but it's very difficult for him."

"Thee moy." The boy cringed. "I can imagine."

"I once read that vampires are a reflection of us. We created the mythology to represent ourselves."

He leaned forward again, his arm almost touching her. "Explain."

She bit her lip, searching for the right words. She must have been thinking hard, for she drew blood. The boy leaned in, and for a moment, she thought he would kiss her.

The bus hit a bump, and she fell back against the window, hitting her head. The boy eased back in his seat. She rubbed her head and turned to face the front.

"You okay?" he asked from behind.

She nodded without looking at him.

"So tell me," he said, leaning on the back of the seat. "How are vampires a reflection of humans?"

"Deep down inside, we're all monsters."

"You really think so?"

She nodded. "And yet we have so little control."

"Power and no power."

She glanced back and gave him a subtle smile. "Exactly."

He said nothing in reply, so she turned to her book. After several minutes, she was finally able to get back into the story. A few times, she wondered about the boy behind her, but she didn't see any reason to try to talk to him. She would be leaving this country in one year, to never return, so what was the use of making friends?

She could hear her mother's voice in the back of her head reminding her that she had no friends at home, either, but it wasn't Gertie's fault that everyone at her private school in New York was fake.

At some point, she must have fallen asleep. When she opened her eyes, she saw the boy leaning over the back of the seat looking down at her with a mouth full of fangs and blood.

She cringed and opened her eyes—for real this time. She glanced back at the boy, but he was gone.

Chapter Two: The Host Family

When she arrived at the station in Athens, she found a boy holding up a sign with her name written on it: Gertrude Morgan. She almost didn't see the sign, because the boy holding it was so beautiful. He was flanked by another boy about his age—eighteen or nineteen, but shorter—and a girl, either the same age or younger.

The girl had studs in her nose and cheek and had spikey, short hair. All three wore summer shorts, flip flops, and t-shirts with graphics of what appeared to be bands. Gertie realized the outer two were related, both having the same brown hair and brown eyes and petite build. They looked nothing like the boy in the middle, who towered over them and was breathtaking, like a Greek god.

"Gertie?" the girl asked as Gertie came to a halt in front of them.

"That's right."

She was astonished when the girl nearly plowed her down with an embrace. "I'm Nikita! It's so great to finally meet you!"

Nikita was the name of one of the members of her host family. She and Gertie had been texting and emailing the past two weeks about the trip—what to bring and what to expect. Surely this girl wasn't one and the same.

"You're Nikita?"

The girl frowned. "This is Hector, our friend. And that's Klaus, my brother. I'm pretty sure I told you all about him. He's been dying to meet you."

"Okay, Nikita," Klaus said. "You don't have to make me sound so eager."

"It's nice to meet you," Gertie said, still a little shocked. They didn't look like the private school kids back home.

"Our parents and little sister are waiting in the car," Nikita said. "Can you boys help her with her bags?"

The two boys took her rolling suitcases—one apiece—and Nikita took one of her shoulder bags, and then they followed the boys through the station to the sidewalk outside. Gertie found herself studying the lines on the back of the taller boy named Hector.

When they reached the car, Gertie had another shock. It was a two-door coupe meant for four passengers, but there were already three inside.

They weren't inside long. Just as Nikita had done, the man, woman, and child, all thin and petite and dark-haired like their other family members, climbed out and hugged her. The mother even kissed her on her cheek.

"We're so glad to have you join our family," the mother said, cupping Gertie's face in her hands. "Look at you, Gertoula! You're so beautiful, koreetsi mou!"

"It's Gertie," Gertie said.

10

"Of course, Gertoula! I mean Gertie."

"Mamá puts oula and itsa and aki on the end of everyone's name. Even Babá's!" Nikita explained. "She calls him Babáki mou!"

"Yes, Nikitsa, koreetsi mou!" her mother said, and turning to Gertie, said, "So you call me Mamá, too. Yes?"

"And I'm Babá," the father said affectionately. Then he picked up his little girl, who seemed seven or eight years old, and said, "And this is Phoebe."

"Mamá calls her Phoeboula, so don't get confused," Klaus said.

"Hello," Gertie said to the girl.

The girl smiled, but said nothing. Then Gertie remembered what Nikita had said in her text about the fire three years ago. Their baby brother had died. Phoebe hadn't spoken since.

Babá and the boys put her luggage in the trunk of the coupe before piling into the car. Phoebe sat in the front seat, without a seatbelt, and Nikita climbed on her brother's lap.

"Should I call a cab?" Gertie asked.

"No, no!" Babá said, holding the door open for her. "There's room for you."

Hector climbed out. "Take my place. I need to head home anyway. I'll take a cab or the bus."

"No, Hector. I promised you baklava," Mamá insisted.

11

"I'll come by for some tomorrow," Hector said. He waved goodbye and then raised his hand for a cab.

Gertie climbed in beside Klaus. Nikita shifted from her brother's lap and squeezed between them. No one wore their seatbelts. Gertie wasn't even sure the old coupe had them.

The car smelled like onions, mold, and sweat, but Gertie resisted pinching her nose as they drove through the streets of Athens from the bus station. Mamá and Babá spoke animatedly about their country, the American school, the ruins, and many other topics during the thirty minute ride. When they pulled up in front of a dilapidated apartment building, Gertie thought they were playing a joke on her.

It wasn't a joke.

Babá and Klaus dragged the heavy suitcases up the three flights of steps to the apartment. Apparently, there were no elevators. When Mamá opened the door and flipped on the light, at least a dozen roaches scrambled for cover.

"Get them!" Babá called.

Nikita dropped Gertie's bag and rushed in behind her brother, stomping like wine-makers in a vat of grapes. Phoebe joined them, enthusiastically, like it was a game.

"Good! Well done!" Babá said as they scooped up the dead bugs with their bare hands and threw them in the garbage can across the room.

Gertie was afraid to step inside.

"Come in! Come in!" Mamá said. "It's not much, but it's very comfortable. No? Let me take your coat. You won't need that here but maybe a few days out of the year."

Gertie kept her coat. "That's all right. Thank you."

The furniture was shabby, but tidy. The kitchen across the room was neat but very outdated. The lighting was poor, which Gertie thought was probably good.

"I'll show you where to put your things," Nikita said. "Let's go."

"And then come back here for my baklava, so Gertoula has a proper welcome," Mamá said.

As they turned down a narrow hall, Nikita said, "That's my brother's room, and my parents have a room down the hall. There's the bathroom, and here is my room, where you'll be staying."

Gertie's face paled. A family of five shared a three-bedroom apartment? The living area and kitchen were tiny, so Gertie had hoped there were bedrooms to escape to. How did everyone fit?

"You can have Phoebe's bed. She'll sleep on a cot with Mamá and Babá while you're here."

"I don't want to be any trouble," Gertie managed to say.

"You must be joking!" Nikita said. "We're all so happy to have you. It's all Mamá and Babá have been talking about. It's been the American girl this and the American girl that for two weeks!"

"I don't understand why they are so happy to have me," Gertie said.

Nikita shrugged. "They are very proud of our country and relish the opportunity to show it off to a young, impressionable American. In other words, they have plans for you every day between now and the start of school. Tomorrow, we go to Crete, Babá's favorite island."

Gertie took in a deep breath. A tiny apartment filled with people and daily activities galore. She wondered when and how she would have time to be alone to read and relax.

She wanted to call her parents and tell them she was sick.

"I'm not feeling well," she said to Nikita. "Can I go straight to bed?"

Nikita's eyes widened. "Oh, no. You just arrived! Mamá and Babá and Klaus and Phoebe—they will all be so disappointed. They've been anxious. I'm sure Mamá has some medicine to make you feel better. Come with me."

Gertie hesitated, so Nikita waited for her in the doorway as Gertie looked around the small bedroom, with its plain white walls and short metal beds. Two scratched-up wooden chests of drawers took up all the wall space between the beds, and there was no on-suite bath—just a small closet without a door, stuffed to the gills with clothes and books.

Gertie stepped closer to the books. "You like to read?"

"Oh, yes. Klaus and I both read voraciously. This is only a small part of our collection. We have many more books downstairs in the basement."

"There's a basement?" Gertie wondered if that might be her getaway.

"It's not very pleasant, but yes. I'll show you tomorrow. Right now, Mamá wants us to eat her dessert."

Chapter Three: The Basement

Gertie had hoped to sleep in, but the walls were thin and the rooms too close to keep the apartment quiet much later than nine o'clock, so she crawled out of bed and asked to use the shower. Because the shower in the main bathroom didn't work, Gertie was forced to use the one in Mamá and Babá's room. Nikita warned her, however, that the toilet in that bathroom was broken, so she should use the one in the hall. So between the two bathrooms there was only one working shower and one working toilet, but plenty of roaches.

"When do we leave for Crete?" Gertie asked Nikita once she had finished dressing and had put on her shoes.

"Not until tonight." Nikita plopped on the rickety bed across from Gertie's. "Want some breakfast?"

"No, thank you. Why tonight?"

"Well, mainly because Babá works all day, but also because it's better to take the ferry while you're sleeping, so you don't waste time."

Great, Gertie thought. Another long ferry ride. She wondered how many people would be sharing her cabin.

"Babá wants us to lunch at his café," Nikita said.

"He owns a café?"

"No, no. He's the cook. He wants to show off his culinary skills. So what do you want to do until then? Hector offered to drive us wherever we want to go. Maybe you want to see the Parthenon?"

"Maybe." She wouldn't mind seeing more of Hector. "But what I'd really like to see is the basement. Before we go sightseeing, will you show me the rest of your books?"

Nikita frowned. "I don't know."

"Please? You were okay with it last night."

Nikita stood up and crossed to the door. "Okay, but don't touch anything."

Gertie followed her out.

When Klaus heard where they were going, he wanted to come too. Mamá begged Gertie to eat something, but Gertie said her stomach was upset.

"Don't touch anything that doesn't belong to you down there," Mamá said to her children as the three teens waved goodbye.

The stairs to the basement were not well-lit, so Gertie held tightly to the railing as her eyes adjusted to the darkness. Once they had made it all the way down, Klaus pulled a chain above his head, and a single bulb illuminated the cavernous room. It was a fairly massive basement, with the dimensions of the building broken up into many nooks and crannies, and entire rooms closed off with heavy wooden doors.

"Our books are over here," Nikita said.

Gertie followed Nikita through a maze of boxes and crates toward a wooden bookshelf against the back wall. Along the way, Gertie noticed two chests in the middle of the room resembling antique coffins. One was as large as a man, and the other half its size.

"Are those what I think they are?" Gertie asked. Heavy chains and padlocks wrapped around the middle of both coffins.

"Of course," Nikita said. "But they don't have dead bodies in them." She laughed—nervously, it seemed to Gertie. "Just a bunch of old stuff."

"How old are these?" Gertie touched the top of the one nearest her.

"No!" Klaus grabbed her hand. "Don't touch that."

Gertie lifted her brows with surprise. "Why not?"

Klaus was still holding Gertie's hand. He dropped it, blushed, and averted his eyes.

"There really are bodies in them, aren't there?" Gertie said without inflection.

"Yes," Klaus said. "So leave them alone."

Nikita narrowed her eyes at her brother. "He's joking."

"Why are they kept down here?" Gertie asked. "Instead of a cemetery?"

Klaus turned to Nikita. "We should tell her."

"Shut *up*, Klaus!" Nikita gave him a threatening glare.

"Tell me what?"

"She's going to find out sooner or later," Klaus insisted.

"We are *not* having this conversation. It will gross her out." Nikita turned to Gertie. "Just ignore him. He wants to frighten you with old stories about the dead, but they are *just* ghost stories."

"I love ghost stories," Gertie said, brightening. "I'm especially fond of vampires."

Nikita clapped a hand to her forehead and closed her eyes. "Can we just look at the books and leave?"

Gertie moved closer to the book shelf and read the titles along the spines. Many of the books were in Greek, but at least a third of them were in English. Of the English books, most were children's classics, such as *The Secret Garden, Charlotte's Web, Huckleberry Finn, Little Women, Island of the Blue Dolphins,* and *Treasure Island*—all of which Gertie had already read. They also had the Harry Potter books, all Rick Riordan books, most of Tolkien's works, and—of all things—all ten books of Anne Rice's *The Vampire Chronicles.*

"Have you read these?" Gertie asked.

"We've read everything down here," Klaus replied.

"I'm on the first one." Gertie plucked the dusty paperback from its place on the shelf and cracked it open. "I have it on my e-reader."

"You're welcome to borrow anything you see," Klaus said.

"Any *book* you see," Nikita qualified. "Most of this stuff down here doesn't belong to us."

"So which one of you is the vampire lover?" Gertie asked, as she returned the book to its shelf.

Before the siblings could answer, a loud noise, like the sound of a thud, startled all three of them.

And it came from the smaller of the two coffins.

All three looked first at the coffin, and then at each other with shocked and terrified eyes. No one breathed for a full five seconds.

Then Klaus said, "Let's get out of here."

The teens scrambled up the basement stairs.

In the doorway, Gertie said, "The light."

"Leave it," Klaus said. "Let's go."

Chapter Four: The Parthenon

After lunch at Babá's café, where the only thing Gertie recognized was the gyro (so that's what she ate), Hector drove Gertie, Nikita, and Klaus to see the Parthenon and other ancient sites.

He drove a red and white Mini Cooper—not what she expected for a boy of his stature, because he seemed too big for it. But it was in good condition, and the four of them fit comfortably. Klaus and Nikita insisted that she take the front seat so she had the better view of the sights as they drove toward the acropolis.

"Why didn't you take your car to the bus station last night?" she asked Hector out of curiosity.

"Mr. and Mrs. Angelis didn't want me to waste my gas when we were going to the same place."

"That's their way," Klaus said.

"Mamá and Babá can be very persuasive," Nikita added.

"So what made you decide to come to Greece?" Hector asked.

Gertie shrugged. "I didn't decide. My mom did."

"Is she from Greece?" he asked.

"No. She came to school here for a year, just before she married my dad. She loved it so much that she wanted me to come, too."

"You'll love it," Nikita said. "Greece is the most beautiful place in the world."

Gertie wished she cared more about seeing beautiful places, but, the truth was, she'd rather read. The adventures in books were always so much more interesting than the ones in real life—though she had to admit that if Hector lived in New York City, she wouldn't mind having an adventure with him. Too bad he lived here.

"It's especially beautiful at night," Klaus said. "We have to take her to the rock to watch the sunset."

"Don't we have to catch the ferry to Crete?" Gertie asked.

"At ten-thirty," Nikita said. "We have plenty of time."

"It can be dangerous here at night," Hector said. "But I guess if we stay together, we'll be all right."

"Dangerous how?" Gertie asked. "You mean like muggers?"

Hector glanced in his rearview mirror at the siblings in the backseat, but they kept their mouths clamped shut.

"Just stay with *me*." Hector reached over and patted her hand, sending shocks of energy up her arm. "And you'll be fine."

Hector squeezed the car into a spot on the side of the road, and then they walked in the summer heat up toward the acropolis. The first thing they came upon was the Theater of Dionysus wedged in the southern slope of the hill.

"Dionysus?" Gertie perked up. "I thought the Parthenon was a tribute to Athena."

"That happened after," Hector said. "This area was first occupied by a cult of Dionysus. This is where drama is said to have been born."

Although Gertie wasn't a fan of sightseeing, she was a fan of the ancient Greeks and their mythology. She loved it almost as much as she did vampire lore.

"There used to be a temple for him here, too," Nikita added. "But it got moved when they built the Parthenon."

"Some people believe that Dionysus continues to hang out here, beneath the acropolis, in the secret caves," Klaus added.

"Secret caves?" Gertie asked. She'd much rather see the secret caves than the broken old buildings.

Nikita and Hector both rolled their eyes at Klaus.

"Come on." Hector continued along the path.

Gertie caught up to him. "Can we go see the caves?"

"They're closed off to tourists," Hector said. "And they're dangerous, so no."

When they passed the area leading up to the Parthenon, Gertie stopped. "Don't we want to go this way?" It was the way everyone else was going.

"Later, before sunset," Nikita said.

"I want to show you the Temple of Hephaestus," Hector said. "It's the best preserved ancient temple in the world."

"And it's special to him, too," Klaus added.

Hector sighed and Nikita shook her head.

"Special how?" Gertie asked.

"Let's go get something to drink." Nikita slapped her brother on the arm. "It's too hot out here."

As they continued down the path, passing an enormous amphitheater they called the Odeon, Klaus said, "You guys are only postponing the inevitable."

Gertie stopped just as they were turning onto a pedestrian street. "What are you talking about, Klaus? What are they not telling me?"

Nikita stepped in front of her brother and squared herself to Gertie. "Hector was born there. He's embarrassed by the story, but Klaus doesn't know how to keep his mouth shut."

"Oh." Gertie followed them along the street toward a stretch of shops and cafés.

The teens were shining with sweat by the time they sat down and ordered drinks. Gertie asked for a Coke. Hector ordered a Frappe. Nikita and Klaus ordered water and insisted on paying the bill. But Hector pulled out his wallet and handed money to the waitress before either of the other two.

"You should let me pay for everything," Gertie said after the waitress had left. "My parents gave me a credit card with unlimited credit."

Nikita and Klaus turned red.

"But you're our guest," Klaus said. "We want to pay."

"Yes, but..." Gertie was about to say that her parents had so much more money than theirs, but she bit her lip. "You are already having me in your home. I want to give something back."

The Angelis kids smiled. *Faux pas* averted.

"Maybe next time," Hector said.

They took their drinks with them as they walked down the road toward the temple. It was a fifteen minute walk, but the heat shining down on them and reflecting up from the pavement made it seem longer.

"Helios is bright today," Hector said.

Gertie smiled. "The sun god, right?"

"She knows Helios!" Klaus said laughing. "This is great."

"I know about all the Greek gods and goddesses," Gertie said. "I love them almost as much as I do vampires."

Hector flinched at her last statement but then tried to cover it up. As they walked further, however, he couldn't seem to resist asking, "How can anybody love vampires?"

"I meant I'm interested in the lore. I love reading stories about them." She told him about *The Vampire Chronicles* and some of the other novels she had read that had made her want to read Anne Rice. "Klaus and Nikita have the whole collection in their basement." Then she added, "That basement is pretty creepy, by the way. We'll have to ask Babá to get me the rest of the books." She laughed.

But Hector's face was serious when he asked, "What happened in the basement?"

"We heard a noise," Gertie said. "In one of the coffins."

"It was probably just a rat," Nikita said, avoiding Gertie's eyes.

"But that coffin is heavily chained," Gertie objected. "How would it have gotten inside?"

"Rats can eat through just about anything," Hector said. "Oh, look. See the temple over there?"

They couldn't get to it from that side, so they had to go around to the east for a few more minutes. Once they reached the ruin, Gertie thought it was worth the walk. It looked exactly as it must have once appeared in ancient Greece, except for a few cracks. Standing in the same spot where others once stood thousands of years ago was surreal.

After they walked around and read some of the plaques, Hector returned to the front of the temple and sat on the ledge looking out over the landscape below.

"See that jumble of rocks down there?" he asked.

Gertie sat beside him and looked down the hill at a maze of stones in the grassy hillside.

"That's the ancient agora," he said.

Nikita and Klaus joined them on the ledge.

Nikita said, "It was like the town square of ancient Greece."

"It's where our ancestors would go to have fun," Klaus said.

Hector laughed. "Like all they did back then was party."

They all laughed.

"They had to have fun some time," Klaus said.

As an American, that was one thing Gertie didn't have: because her ancestors were immigrants, she couldn't walk around in her hometown and reflect on the ancient past of her heritage. She had to go to another country to do that.

Gertie really wanted to ask Hector to tell the story about the day he was born, but she didn't know him well enough, and she didn't want to embarrass him. She supposed she would have to coax the details out of Nikita later.

They spent the rest of the afternoon walking around the acropolis and then had some dinner at one of the cafés. Gertie was able to convince them to let her pay with her credit card. At seven in the evening, they climbed the hill up to the Parthenon. Most of the other tourists were leaving to catch their buses and ferries and taxis, but there were still some milling about and enjoying the drop in temperature on the now windy hill.

They walked around inside, all three of them inundating Gertie with information, and then Klaus called everyone outside.

"Let's climb down to the rock," he said. "The sun is close to setting."

"Don't you mean Helios is about to sink in his cup?" Gertie teased.

"Wait," Nikita said. "First Hector should tell Gertie about his great-grandfather. It happened right here."

"What happened right there?" Gertie asked.

"Oh, okay," Hector said. "But first, look over there. That's where Athena and Poseidon had their famous contest over who would become the patron god of this city. Have you heard the story?"

Gertie nodded. "That's where it happened, huh? Poseidon gave them a salty river and Athena the olive tree. So where's the olive tree?"

"They're all over this area," Hector replied. "We have the best olive oil in the world."

"Now you sound like Babá," Nikita said.

"But it's true," Hector argued.

"Can we go to the rock now?" Klaus asked.

"Wait, his great-grandfather's story," Nikita prompted. "Go ahead, Hector."

Gertie was beginning to get the feeling that Nikita was in love with Hector.

"Oh, right," Hector said. "Well, during World War II, the Nazis occupied Athens."

Klaus came over and put an arm around Gertie. "And his great-grandfather was guarding the Greek flag when the Nazis ordered him to take it down."

Klaus was the same height as Gertie, and he looked at her, eye-to-eye with a cute smile on his face. She hadn't noticed his deep dimples before. Was he flirting with her? Or just being friendly, like Mamá and Babá and Nikita?

"So did he take it down?" Gertie asked Hector.

"He did," Hector said. "He took it down, put it on, like a badge of courage, and jumped to his death, right down there."

"He was standing on this very spot. Right, Hector?" Nikita said.

Hector nodded.

"Can we go to the rock now?" Klaus, who still had his arm around Gertie, asked.

"Let's go," Hector said, leading the way.

They climbed down from the flag platform onto a dimpled, raw ledge of rock jetting out from the acropolis just below the Parthenon. According to Nikita, teenagers liked to come hang out here some evenings, sometimes with an iced chest of beer or bottle of wine to share—always in groups and never alone. Tonight, there were no others, and the few tourists above them were already making their way down along the path on the other side of the hill.

Every part of Athens was visible from this spot except the west, but the view of the sun dipping down behind the Parthenon from here was spectacular. She sat between Klaus and Nikita, with Hector on the other side of Klaus, all dangling their legs over the cliff edge. It was peaceful and beautiful up here, as the tiled rooftops sparkled in the evening sun and the lights of the city slowly began to twinkle as dusk settled.

The city below was not quite sleepy, however. Gertie could see cars, people, smoke from chimney tops, and lots of other signs of human activity. She looked at her phone for the time.

"I thought this place closed at eight-thirty," she said.

"We can climb down from here," Klaus said, showing his dimples, apparently happy for the adventure.

"Too bad Dionysus can't come out and bring us some of his wine," Gertie said with a laugh. "Thanks a lot for giving me ideas, Nikita. I'm thirsty now."

The other three didn't laugh, so Gertie added, "Just joking." She thought Europeans were more open-minded about the drinking age; maybe she was wrong.

They were quiet then as the wind lifted their hair in its breeze and cooled them down.

That's when Gertie noticed two people climbing up from the hillside toward them.

Hector stood up. "Don't say anything to them when they come by."

Gertie bent her brows. They'd been surrounded by people all day. What made these two any different?

"And don't make eye contact with them." Klaus stood up too.

Gertie gave Nikita a quizzical look.

"They're tramps," she whispered. "They just want to take advantage of you."

"How can you tell?" Gertie asked.

The boy and girl making their way up toward them didn't look much different from anyone else. They wore summer tanks and blue jeans and had dark, wavy hair. They looked like brother and sister, but were thicker and taller in stature than the Angelis kids.

As the two hikers climbed closer, Gertie's brows shot up even higher. She recognized one of them. He was the boy from the bus.

The boy noticed her, too, and smiled.

"The girl from the bus," he said. "The vampire lover."

"Vampire lover?" the girl beside him asked.

Hector helped Gertie and Nikita to their feet. Then he positioned himself between them and the newcomers. Klaus stood beside him.

"This is my sister, Calandra," the boy said, ignoring Hector. "Calandra, this is...sorry, I didn't get your name."

"Don't answer," Hector muttered. "Xasoy apo ta matia moy."

"It's okay," Gertie said. "I've talked with him before."

"But you don't understand, Gertie," Klaus said.

Hector turned to Klaus. "Way to go."

"Gertie? Nice to meet you. I'm Jeno."

He gave her his brilliant smile, and she was suddenly reminded of the dream she'd had on the bus, of him looming

31

over her with his mouth full of fangs and blood. She shuddered, but, out of habit, said, "It's nice to meet you."

"We were just leaving," Hector said, pulling the girls down the hill in the opposite direction.

Klaus followed closely behind.

"I hope we meet again!" Jeno called after them.

Gertie couldn't understand how the friendliest people on the planet could be so rude, but she waited until they were at the bottom of the hillside, on the street, walking back toward the car, to bring it up.

"They seemed nice," she said. "I don't understand why we had to leave."

"We need to get to the ferry anyway," Nikita said.

Hector stopped abruptly and turned, looking down at her with his face fierce and close to hers. "Never talk to them again, okay?"

"But why?" she asked.

"Trust me," Hector said, his breath washing against her face.

"But I've just met you." She narrowed her eyes. "In fact, I met Jeno before I met you. That means I've known him longer. Give me a reason why I shouldn't talk to him."

"Because he's dangerous," Klaus said.

The muscles of Hector's jaw tightened. "Dangerous and selfish. He'll try to hurt you."

Chapter Five: Close Quarters

"So you four take that one," Babá said in the hallway of the ferry, "and Phoebe and Mamá and I will sleep here."

"Girls on top, boys on bottom," Mamá added, which caused all four teens to snicker.

Babá's face turned bright red, and he smiled sheepishly, but Mamá just bent her brows and asked, "What?"

The four-bed cabin had no window, and the beds were like coffins with no more than two feet between them. The top bunks were bolted onto the wall and folded up when they weren't being used. Since the teens weren't sleepy, they left the top beds folded and sat across from one another—girls on one bed and boys on another—utterly awkward and bored until Nikita begged Hector to play his ukulele.

"What if I didn't pack it?" Hector asked.

"No way," Nikita challenged. "You never go on journeys without it."

"You got me there," he said with a smile. He pulled a bag out from under one of the beds. "Let me just unzip this here and get out the ol' instrument then."

The other three broke into hysterical laughter.

"You're worse than Mamá!" Klaus cried. Tears had come to his eyes from laughing so hard.

Gertie fell back on the bed, forgetting how narrow it was, and hit her head on the cabin wall. This brought more laughter from the bunch, including Gertie, who didn't mind the brief smart to her skull.

Hector played traditional songs that all of them knew, except Gertie. She listened to them sing in Greek. Then they taught her some of the words. It was all rubbish to her, until they translated it, and even then, it was still rubbish.

"What does that mean, 'four winds took them on a promenade'?" she asked them.

They laughed and shrugged, until Hector said, "Chance was dancing with them. See?"

"But none of it makes sense when you put it all together," Gertie said. "Gilded words for the next generation, going down to Hades. I don't get it."

"You'll get it someday," Klaus said sagely.

"My young padawan," Nikita giggled.

As much as Gertie laughed at them, she had to admit that all three of them had lovely voices. It was obvious they sang together often, because they were able to harmonize. When Gertie asked if they were in choir or a band, they said no, not yet.

"We will be," Nikita said. "In school this year."

Around midnight, Babá knocked on the door and told them all to go to bed, so they did. They took turns using the toilet in the tiny closet. Gertie couldn't stop giggling as she lay on her bunk thinking how she was "sleeping on top of Hector." She cupped her hand to her mouth and tried to stop.

Eventually, she pulled her e-reader from her bag and read the last chapters of *Interview with a Vampire* as the others snored.

At some point, after she had finished the book and had nearly dozed off, she heard Hector get up and leave the cabin. She looked at the time on her phone. Four in the morning? Where would he be going at four in the morning?

She left her phone and e-reader beneath her pillow and climbed from her bed to follow him.

In her bare feet, she crept along the narrow hallway. Hector was nowhere in sight. Worried she might be sleep walking, she pinched herself. No. She was definitely not asleep.

When she reached the top of the steps leading to the deck, the wind railed against her, sending her hair in all directions. Despite the wind, the night sky was clear and full of stars. The moon was full, bathing the deck in light.

She glanced around and finally saw Hector twenty feet away, leaning against the rail, looking out to sea. His pale skin, blond hair, and white t-shirt and boxers made him easy to spot in the moonlight. Gertie realized her own blonde hair, white night shirt, and purple shorts made her equally conspicuous, but she didn't care. All she cared about was learning what had prompted Hector to come. Had he needed fresh air? Maybe he couldn't sleep.

The sea air was amazingly refreshing. For a moment, Gertie closed her eyes and took a deep breath. Then she clutched the rail and looked out at the ocean and the distant land, both twinkling with lights. The reflection of the stars on the sea resembled flittering fireflies, and the lights on the land in the distance a fireworks show. Gertie was grateful to see it.

She was startled by a couple making out in the corner— at least she hoped they were just making out. She crept past them and headed toward Hector.

The wind made it impossible to hear anything, so there was no use calling his name. She glanced up to the bridge and couldn't see anyone manning the ferry—though she was sure someone had to be there steering it. She continued toward Hector and was about four feet behind him when he did something that completely shocked her: He climbed over the railing and flung himself into the sea.

Gertie's mouth dropped open and she ran to the rail, searching the waters for his pale head. It emerged but was many yards away by now as the ferry rolled onward. She glanced back up at the bridge, hoping an adult had seen him jump, but no horn blasted, no voice shouted, nothing.

Not knowing what to do, she hollered out for help. "Man overboard!"

Maybe the couple would hear her. She even looked for them. They were no longer on deck. Not knowing what else to do, she climbed onto the rail and jumped in after Hector.

The water was ice cold! And she immediately regretted her stupid, stupid decision to jump. What could *she* do? She was at least a hundred yards away from Hector. She'd never find him in this enormous sea, and the boat was disappearing fast.

Plus the waves were much bigger than they had appeared from on board the ferry. From the bottom of a swell, she could see nothing but a wall of water in front of her, and then she was lifted up, higher and higher, and could see the signs of land and of civilization by their twinkling lights. But then she was down, deep, at the bottom of another swell, hopelessly treading water and getting nowhere.

All she could think was what a stupid, stupid girl she was.

"I panicked," she muttered. "They'll come back for us. Eventually."

It might be hours before anyone would wake up and notice, but she tried to think optimistically. She and Hector would be found. They *would* be. They *had* to be.

Maybe Hector didn't want to be found. Why else would he jump? He hadn't seemed depressed or suicidal. Gertie's mind reeled.

Then she began to think of all the creatures in the water below her and was seized by terror. In all the *Discovery* and *Animal Planet* shows she had ever watched, getting attacked by sharks was never a pleasant experience.

Once she awoke from the shock, she screamed, "Hector! Hector!"

She knew he was too far away to hear her, but what else could she do alone in the middle of the dark sea with creatures swimming beneath her, ready to eat her alive?

"Hector!"

Then she noticed something moving toward her in the water—something big and fast. She saw no dorsal fin, but that didn't mean it wasn't a shark.

She screamed.

The thing stopped, and a pale head surfaced. It flung wet hair back from its face and looked at her with bright blue eyes.

"Gertie?"

She stared at the creature for several seconds before she realized it was Hector.

"Gertie, what are you doing out here? Are you crazy?"

She opened and closed her chattering jaw several times, but couldn't find the words. Did he realize what he was saying?

He moved closer and put his arms around her. "You're going to be okay."

"You jumped," she finally said.

"I didn't know anyone was following me."

"But why?"

He used his body to attempt to warm her trembling limbs. "I, um, was in the mood for a swim."

She narrowed her eyes at him.

Chapter Six: The Crane

"What do you mean you were in the mood for a swim? You're the one who's crazy," she said.

He smiled and pulled her close. Now that more of the shock had worn off, she was aware of his strong, hard body against hers.

"What's going on?" she demanded.

"I'm a fast swimmer," he said. "I would have caught up with the boat."

She pushed away from him. "Are you insane?"

He laughed and turned a little red. "No. I'm not. But I don't think I can catch up to it towing you."

He pulled her close, turned her back to him, and then wrapped an arm across her chest, like a beauty pageant sash. She flailed her arms, fighting him, but it did no good. Before she could say one word, he took off swimming, as fast as a dolphin, with her back against his chest.

The ocean swells continued to lift them up and set them down in the night sky, but now they were moving as fast as a tug boat toward the island of Crete.

This did not gel with anything Gertie knew about the universe, and within seconds she was totally freaked out. The only thing she could think to do was to scream.

Hector stopped. "What's wrong?"

Where could she begin?

"I think I *am* the one who's crazy," she muttered through chattering lips.

He turned her around to face him.

"I'm having some kind of hallucination," she said. "Maybe someone drugged me."

She touched his face, to see if it felt real. It did. She cupped his face in both of her hands and studied him. "Are you real?"

He wasn't smiling anymore. His face took on a serious expression as his gaze fell upon her mouth.

"Yes, I am," he whispered as he covered her lips with his.

What a strange night, Gertie thought, as she closed her eyes and sank into his arms. She kissed him back, with the attitude that if she was going to have a hallucination, it may as well be a good one. If this had been real, she would have pulled away, out of respect for Nikita's obvious feelings, but it wasn't. Although she didn't know how to kiss, he seemed to be doing just fine with her inexperience as he slid his soft, wet, luscious lips across hers.

"I'm sorry," he said, lifting his head and avoiding her eyes. "I…"

"I'm not," she said bravely—it was a hallucination, so what did it matter what she said? "I liked it."

He smiled at her. "Look at you. You're freezing. I'll call my dad for help."

Of course, there was no way he could do such a thing. First, even if he *did* have a phone on him somewhere (and where exactly would that be? In his boxers?), it would be ruined by now. Second, what could his father do to help them? Fly a copter overhead and launch a rope ladder down to them?

"This is such a strange hallucination," she muttered. "But okay, call your dad."

Hector closed his eyes and lifted his face toward the stars.

She studied the fine lines of his forehead, cheeks, nose, and jaw. She wanted to reach out and trace her finger along his solid neck, Adam's apple, and chest. "And why shouldn't I?" she whispered to herself as she shivered with the cold water splashing against her. So she touched his jaw and felt the skin along his neck. She felt the pectoral muscles of his chest beneath the t-shirt. He opened his eyes and looked at her, as though he, too, were in a trance. She moved her hands to his hard abs and encircled his waist. She was about to continue her hands' journey down his backside, when he grabbed her arms, cleared his throat, and pointed to the sky.

An enormous white bird flew toward them, its long neck outstretched, its wings moving gracefully through the wind. It swooped down and grasped hold of each of them—one in each of its claws, wrapped firmly around their waists.

41

Gertie screamed and flailed wildly through the air.

"Gertie, it's okay!" Hector shouted. "Relax! Relax and enjoy the ride!"

She stopped flailing and looked around.

They sailed twenty feet above the sea, side by side in the claws of the giant crane. The bird carried them in the direction of the ferry and the island of Crete. Gertie shook her head, wondering what she had ingested, and who had given it to her. She'd never experienced anything like this before.

Hector reached out and held her hand. She returned his smile and began to laugh. This was so crazy. She was so crazy. But it was also amazing. She may as well enjoy.

Within minutes, the ferry came into view. Gertie glanced over at Hector and laughed.

"Woo-hoo!" he shouted. "Isn't this great?"

"It's amazing!" she shouted. "Incredible!"

The crane hovered over the deck. Gertie looked through the windows of the bridge for sign of a captain. She thought she saw someone bent over a control panel. She couldn't be sure.

"Get ready!" Hector shouted. "We'll have to jump."

"What? Are you serious?" Then she laughed, because she kept forgetting none of this was real. "Okay! Just say when!"

"Don't forget to roll!" he said, squeezing her hand. "On the count of three."

She nodded, waiting, as the bird hovered over the deck.

"One, two, three!" Hector cried, and the bird released them.

Their hands fell apart as they landed on the deck. Her hip and shoulder hit hard against the boat. She forgot to roll. She hadn't thought it mattered, but now she was in pain.

Hector looked down at her, where she lay sprawled on the back of the boat. "Are you okay?"

Gertie closed her eyes. Everything hurt. This must be where the hangover would begin.

She blinked to find herself in Hector's arms as he maneuvered down the steps below deck and through the narrow hallway to their cabin. Except for the heat from his body, she was colder now than she'd been in the sea, and she shivered uncontrollably. Hector opened the door of their cabin and laid her down on his bottom bunk. He helped her from her wet clothes and wrapped her tightly in the blankets. She was so sleepy, tired, and dazed, that she went through the motions, only partially aware.

Then he climbed out of his own wet clothes, slipped on dry ones, and crawled in beside her. He held her in his arms, and whispered, "Try to get some sleep. I'll explain everything tomorrow."

Her body rejoiced at the warmth and coziness enfolding it, so she did as Hector said and closed her eyes. Behind her lids, she saw the big, beautiful, white crane flying across the dark night.

Chapter Seven: The Island of Crete

"Gertie?" someone murmured near Gertie's ear.

She blinked, opened her eyes, and looked up. This was not the same place she had gone to sleep the night before. She felt beneath her pillow for her e-reader and phone, and came up empty. Her arms wrapped themselves around her shoulders only to find no clothes between them and the rest of her.

"Where are my clothes?"

Clinging to the covers, which surrounded her like a burrito, she turned in the bed to see Hector lying beside her. Her hip, shoulder, and head hurt, but the sight of him beside her made adrenaline surge through her body, numbing it. What she had taken for a hallucination last night must have been, in part, real. Obviously a giant bird hadn't swooped down and lifted her and Hector from the sea, but maybe they had made out. He had removed her clothes. Had he also drugged her?

"They're still wet," he said.

"Why are they wet?" she demanded. "And what did you do?"

She moved as far away from him in the bed as possible, clutching the covers around her otherwise naked body.

"Will you both be quiet?" Nikita said from her top bunk. "It's not time to get up yet."

"Don't you remember?" Hector whispered.

"Did you drug me?" She made no attempt to keep her voice down. Anger flared through her.

His jaw dropped open and he flinched.

Klaus lifted his sleepy head from his pillow, just two feet away. "What's going on over there?"

"Hector?" Gertie said. "Can you explain?"

His mouth hung open for a few more seconds before he said, "I thought we had a beautiful night together, but I guess I was wrong."

He climbed from the bed and went to the closet to use the toilet.

Klaus stared at Gertie. "What happened?"

She shrugged as heat flooded to her face. "I honestly don't know."

"You don't make sense," Klaus said, falling back on his pillow.

"I think he drugged me," she whispered.

Klaus laughed. "Hector would never do such a thing."

"Could you hand me my bag? It's on the foot of my bed."

Klaus reluctantly crawled from his bunk just as Hector was returning from the toilet. The cabin grew silent as the two boys stood beside one another between the beds. Gertie thought they were exchanging looks, maybe even whispers, but she couldn't see their faces to know for sure. Klaus handed over her bag as Hector climbed into a pair of jeans. Babá knocked on the door and told everyone to wake up.

"We go first to Lion Square for Bhougatsa and coffee," Babá said through the door.

Gertie spent the day ignoring Hector as best as she could without being too noticeable to the rest of the family. She didn't want to ruin everyone else's fun after all the trouble they had gone to, and she certainly didn't want Nikita to know what may or may not have happened.

Only one thing was perfectly clear to Gertie: she had awakened in Hector's bed without a stitch of clothes on her body.

The city of Heraklion was not what she had expected, and not what she had hoped to see. Except for the fountains, it looked just like any other modern city with its congested streets and busy sidewalks. Babá took them from one restaurant to another, bragging about the food, how it was the best and the freshest in the world. He also bought several bottles of local olive oil, honey, and some spices he said you couldn't get anywhere else.

Mamá wanted them to see some of the museums, which were even more boring than the restaurants. It wasn't until they took a cab to the palace ruins of Knossos that Gertie perked up.

She already knew the stories of King Minos and the Minotaur, of Daedalus and the labyrinth. She also knew the story of Icarus, who flew too close to the sun, melting the wax holding together the wings built for him by his father before falling into the sea to his death.

It was amazing to stand among the ruins of all those old stories and imagine the characters and their lives. The legends had to be based on some truth, after all.

Hector seemed to notice her change of mood, and when she was standing alone, gazing at a painting of a bull, he came up behind her and said, "Pretty incredible, huh?"

She nodded without looking at him, the awkward feelings returning with his presence.

"Knossos is the oldest city of Europe," he said. "We're standing on the foundation of modern civilization."

She wished she could forget about what had happened, so she could turn and smile and say how surreal it all was, but she couldn't trust him anymore. She felt betrayed.

"I have a family connection to this place," Hector continued. "My family shares the same bloodline with Daedalus, the person credited for designing..."

"I know who Daedalus was," she interrupted.

"Look," he began. "I don't understand why you're angry with me, or why you would think I would drug you."

She struggled with whether she should admit everything she had imagined to the person who may have caused it. "I had a strange vision last night. Like a hallucination. I must have ingested something. I thought maybe you..."

His face paled. Then the muscles in his jaws flexed, like he was holding something back. "No. I didn't."

Before she had a chance to ask how she had ended up in his bed, he walked away without another word.

Later, while she was following the maze of the ruins and imagining the Minotaur and Ariadne and Theseus, and also the seven boys and girls sent from Athens every year to be eaten by the Minotaur, Nikita came up behind her.

"Hey, Gertie. Are you doing okay?"

She waited for Nikita to catch up to her. "I'm fine."

They traced the maze of the ruins together in silence until Nikita asked, "Are we overwhelming you with all this sightseeing? You must be tired."

"I'm fine," she said again.

"You seem quieter today."

"I had strange dreams last night and couldn't sleep."

"Oh."

They walked along in silence again, and then, almost as though she couldn't help herself, Nikita asked, "What kind of strange dreams? Of vampires?"

Gertie decided to tell her what she'd imagined—except for the parts about making out with Hector and waking up in his bed. She had expected Nikita to laugh and agree with how bizarre it sounded, but, instead, Nikita's mouth hung open like a Labrador retriever's.

"Did you say a giant crane?" Nikita asked.

48

"Pretty weird, right?" Gertie kept walking along the path, about to overtake another group of tourists.

Nikita stopped and grabbed Gertie's arm. "Wait."

Gertie searched Nikita's face. "What?"

Nikita waited for a few other tourists to pass them by, and then she said, "Never mind. You're right. That was a bizarre dream."

Gertie was suspicious now that Nikita wasn't being upfront with her. She glanced warily at her new friend wondering just how much she could trust her. A sick feeling in her stomach made her wish she was back home, where at least she knew what to expect from day to day.

Before they caught up with the others in their group, Gertie asked, "Why is Hector embarrassed to talk about the day he was born?"

"I'm not embarrassed," he said from behind her.

She nearly jumped out of her shoes. She had no idea he had been there.

Turning to look at him, she said, "I thought you said you *were*."

"No, Nikita did," he clarified. "She was just saying that to make things easier. I don't like to tell my story to just anyone, and not because it's embarrassing. In fact, it's the opposite of embarrassing. But it's a secret. And I only share it with people I trust."

He brushed past them and caught up with Klaus and the rest of the Angelis family.

Gertie glanced at Nikita, whose face had turned pink.

"What did you say to Hector to make him so angry?" Nikita whispered.

Tears stung Gertie's eyes. "I just want to go home."

Chapter Eight: Lost in the City

The ferry ride home was miserable for Gertie. Everyone went straight to bed, worn out from the sightseeing, but Gertie couldn't fall asleep. To make matters worse, both her phone and her e-reader were dead, and there was no place in the cabin to charge them.

So she lay there thinking of all the things she could say to her parents to get them to let her come home.

By the time they reached the apartment, Gertie could no longer keep her eyes open, so she went to her bed to sleep. It didn't seem like much time had passed when she felt someone nudge her awake.

"Gertoula." Mamá sat on the edge of the bed and patted Gertie's leg. "Did we wear you out, koreetsi mou?"

Gertie sat up and leaned against the metal head board. "I'm okay. I just couldn't sleep on the ferry."

Mamá caressed Gertie's hair in a way Gertie's own mother never had. "You are such a pretty girl. I hope you are happy with us. You seemed sad yesterday in Crete."

"I'm a little homesick," Gertie said, which wasn't *exactly* a lie.

Mamá threw her arms around Gertie. "I am sorry, koreetsi mou. Have you spoken to your parents today?"

"No, ma'am."

"Maybe you should call them." She pulled back from the hug and cupped Gertie's cheeks. "Maybe hearing your mother's voice will cheer you up, yes?"

Gertie doubted that, but she nodded. "I could also use some fresh air." She really just wanted to be alone with her thoughts. "May I go for a walk?"

"Of course you may. Nikita and Klaus would love to show you around after you eat."

"I meant alone, so I can think."

Mamá frowned. "I understand. Yes, of course. But you won't go far? And you won't get lost?"

Gertie brought out her phone. "I have Google Maps."

"Google what?" Mamá looked perplexed.

"My phone will show me the way home." She had plugged it in as soon as they had returned from Crete, and it was fully charged.

"Okay, koreetsi mou, but you must promise to return home before dark. I love my city, and am very proud of its history, but I would wish for no one to walk the streets alone at night."

Gertie nodded. "I promise."

"Eat something first, yes?"

Gertie followed Mamá into the kitchen where the rest of the Angelis family were already sitting around the table, crammed close together. Mamá insisted that Gertie take her chair.

"I like to stand," Mamá said, holding her plate up to her chin.

Although the spices were different from what Gertie was used to, the pork, rice, and vegetables were delicious. She dipped the flat bread into the olive oil and wiped her plate clean. This made Mamá and Babá very happy.

When they had finished eating, Mamá announced, "Nikita and Klaus will help me with the dishes. Gertie wants to go for a walk alone. She's not used to such a big family. Am I right, Gertoula?"

Gertie nodded with a smile.

"I don't blame you," Klaus said. "I try to get away as often as possible, too."

Mamá slapped Klaus with her dish towel and everyone laughed. Gertie could tell Klaus hadn't meant what he had said.

"Be back before dark," Mamá said again. "In thirty minutes, please."

"And avoid Omonoia Square," Babá added.

"That's where the tramps like to hang out," Nikita explained.

"Just stay on this side of Kapodistriou," Klaus called from the kitchen sink.

She knew the direction of the square, because they had passed it on the way to the Parthenon. It didn't seem at all like the kind of place where tramps would hang out after dark. Tall skyscrapers, bustling streets, and a lovely pedestrian walkway at its center seemed way too open to the public for tramps wanting to take advantage of tourists.

And the square hadn't actually been a square. It was a semicircle. As they had driven past, Hector had said something about the "Omonoia Hexagon." And when Gertie had said it was not a hexagon, he had said he'd show her what he meant someday.

She supposed that day would never come since they were no longer speaking to one another.

In spite of everything, Gertie was glad to be out of the apartment and on her own as she followed the sidewalk along the busy street. It wasn't as hot as it had been in the morning, and there was a nice breeze. As she passed people on the sidewalk, most of them smiled at her. A few even said, "Yasou," which she knew meant, "Hello." She wasn't used to this. People didn't do that on the streets of New York City.

When she reached one of the main roads, she turned left, in the opposite direction of the square—or whatever shape people called it.

Although it wasn't cool out, she wished she had her gray puffer coat, because whenever she wore it, she felt like her grandma was with her. It had been the last gift her grandmother had given her before she had passed away.

She prayed to her grandma in silence as she walked the streets, fighting the tears wanting to flow from her eyes. Mamá had said to call her mother, but Gertie was still upset with her parents for making her come to Greece. She spoke to her grandma instead.

It wasn't long before her mind wandered to Hector and what she had imagined with him in the sea. It had been an amazing dream—the best of her life. Why couldn't Hector be honest with her about what had really happened? All of them— even Nikita—were keeping secrets from her, and (unless by some miracle her parents allowed her to go home) she was determined to uncover them.

When she reached a corner and prepared to cross the street, she was shocked to see Omonoia Square in front of her. She stopped and looked up at the tall buildings, turning around in all directions. Hadn't she gone the opposite way? Now she was totally confused. She pulled her phone from her pocket and clicked on Google Maps. An error message popped up in the screen.

"Oh, no!" she muttered beneath her breath.

She tried to open Google Maps again, but received the same error message.

Well, at least she could retrace her steps. She turned around and headed in the same direction she had come. After two blocks, though, nothing looked familiar. She pivoted and went back the other way.

When she reached Omonoia Square again, she took out her phone and called Nikita. The call went straight to voice mail.

She texted: "Help. I'm lost. At Omonoia Square."

She walked up and down the pedestrian path as she waited for Nikita to answer her text. Meanwhile, dusk had fallen.

Just great.

The square was still bustling with people. In fact, more of them emerged from the underground subway and strolled along the sidewalks and streets, where fewer cars drove by. Gertie thought she could see the acropolis in the fading light. If so, she *really had* been turned around.

She headed in the opposite direction of the acropolis in what she thought must be the way back to Nikita's apartment, when a woman stepped in her way and asked, "Are you lost?"

The woman's blonde hair fell to her shoulders. She smelled bad and wore very outdated clothing, but her face was young and beautiful.

"No, ma'am," Gertie said.

"I was watching you," the woman said. "I believe you are lost. May I help you find your way? Elate mazi moy."

Another beautiful woman, taller and thinner than the first with short black hair and darker skin, came up beside them. "Na sas bohthhsw?"

Gertie shook her head. "I don't speak Greek."

A third woman came from around the corner. She wore a long scarf over her head. She was also beautiful, but not as young as the other two. "Let me help her. It's my turn to *help*."

A group of men shouted from the center of the square.

"Ela thou!" they hollered. "Trexa!"

56

"Prosexe!" said another.

She peered over the shoulders of the women surrounding her to see a group—some standing, some sitting—on the pavement in the center of the pedestrian path of the square.

"Here!" one voice rang out in English. "Over here!"

They looked like a group of homeless people, so why were they calling out to her? Was she so obviously rich?

"Don't listen to them," one of the women said. "Come with us, darling girl."

"We'll share," the tallest one said.

"Look into my eyes," said the one with the scarf.

Her phone buzzed. With a shaky hand, she pulled it from her pocket. The text from Nikita read, "Get to the center of the square NOW!!!"

The tallest of the three women took Gertie by the arm just as she was about to make a run for it.

"Where are you going, darling?" the blonde woman asked. "Don't be in such a hurry. Elate mazi moy."

"Leave me alone!" Gertie shouted.

She tried to break free of the woman's grip, but couldn't. All three women moved in closer. Gertie couldn't breathe.

"Don't touch her!" came a familiar voice. "She's *mine*!"

The women hissed as Gertie was ripped from their clutches. Gertie looked up to see the face of her savior.

"Jeno?"

"Come with me. Quickly."

Chapter Nine: Jeno

"Where are we going?" Gertie asked, as Jeno led her across the semicircle of Omonoia Square.

"The subway. It's safer for you there."

They took the steps underground. Jeno used his card to get them through the turnstile. They had barely reached the platform when the train arrived, and its doors swooshed open.

"But the Angelis family will be worried," Gertie protested.

"I'll get you home safely," Jeno said. "I promise."

Gertie followed him onto the train and sat beside him next to the window in an otherwise empty car. The bright lights brought out more of the beauty in Jeno's features, especially his dark eyes.

"I should text Nikita." Gertie took out her phone and wrote, "I'm okay. On the subway, heading home."

"It seems you and I and public transportation—we have a thing going, no?" Jeno laughed.

Gertie laughed, too. "Those women gave me the creeps. Thanks for helping me."

"Your friend hasn't educated you about our city," Jeno said.

"She and her family are working on it. We went to Crete yesterday. Heraklion."

"I have relatives there. Did you see Knossos?"

"My favorite part."

"I like you," Jeno said. "You're different."

She liked him, too. "You don't meet many Americans?"

"I meet *many* Americans, but none as interesting as you," he said. "You're the first vampire lover, anyway."

She blushed. "They make for interesting stories."

"What if I told you the stories are true?" Jeno said, leaning close.

Gertie laughed. "You're funny." His gorgeous eyes and beautiful smile were intoxicating.

"I'm not trying to be funny."

Gertie bit her lip. What was he getting at?

"Those women back there..." he started.

"Were they tramps?" Gertie asked.

"That's one word for them. Tramps, vamps..."

Gertie's brows shot up. "Did you say *vamps*?"

"Those words are pretty much interchangeable in Athens for those who speak English," he said calmly. "The vamps are the tramps of the city. It's because we have no economic resources available to us. We have no choice but to live in the caves beneath the acropolis."

Gertie's body stiffened. She opened her mouth, but no words came out.

"I have relatives in Knossos who live in caves beneath the palace ruins," he continued. "We have no choice because there are no jobs for us. No one will hire us, and we can only work at night."

"Wait a minute," Gertie said. "Are you saying *vamps*? As in *vampires*?"

"In Greek, they say vrykolakas, and vryks for short, which sometimes gets translated to freaks. Others call us zitiános, which means beggar." Jeno looked at her with a smile and winked. "You're different because you understand us. We don't choose to be the way we are. And you said so yourself, we're not really any different from humans. We may use people for blood, but humans use one another all the time for different things. And we don't kill intentionally. It's against the rules. Humans intentionally kill one another all the time."

"If you're trying to freak me out, you're doing a good job," Gertie said. "Be serious, now. Those women back there wanted my money."

"Not your money—though if you had offered them some, they wouldn't have turned you down. Like I said, we have no economic resources. But they weren't after your money."

She bit her lip, and when the taste of blood reached her tongue, Jeno looked longingly at her mouth.

"You smell so good," he said softly.

When he met her eyes, she felt drawn to him. He mesmerized her. She blinked and pulled herself to her senses. "If they weren't after my money, then what?"

"Your blood," he said.

"What?"

"They need it to survive. Like you said, they can't help themselves."

Gertie jumped to her feet and climbed over his legs to the other side of the car. "You're scaring me." He must be crazy, she thought. She would get off at the next stop.

"That's not a good idea," he said. "It's not safe on the streets of Athens after dark. And I'm not crazy."

Could he read her mind?

"Yes," he said. "I can."

She held her breath as her heart went wild beneath her ribs. She flattened against the wall of the train, as far away from him as possible.

"I won't hurt you," he said. "You have no reason to fear me."

Gertie didn't move. She stared at him in utter horror. "Stay away from me."

"Okay. I promise. I just want to talk to you."

"I want to go home."

"I will take you there. Just give me the address."

"No way."

"Look into my eyes," he said.

How could she not? He was beautiful. She would do anything he asked.

"You need to calm down," he said.

She nodded. "Yes, I need to…wait" she broke her eye contact with him. "I know what you're doing! I'm an expert on vampires, remember?"

"So you finally believe me." He smiled.

The metro-rail slowed down as it entered the station. Gertie jumped to the doors, anxious for them to open.

"I'm getting off here. Don't follow me," she said.

"Vamps are bad here. A few more stops, and I'll walk you home. I promise."

She glared at him. "Why should I believe you?"

"You have little choice."

"I'll take my chances, thank you very much."

As soon as the doors opened, she jumped off the train and made a run for it. When she emerged from the station, she found herself at the acropolis, alone. She took out her phone and dialed Nikita.

From out of nowhere, it seemed, a man came up and spoke to her in Greek. Gertie backed away, toward the station and into the light of the street lamp.

The man was tall and thick with dark blond hair and blue, magnetic eyes. He gave her a menacing smile and said something again. This time, the points of his fangs appeared between his lips.

She froze.

He moved closer—slowly, gracefully, as though he wished to catch a fly.

"She's mine," Jeno hissed from behind her. Then he said something in Greek.

The taller man disappeared into thin air.

Gertie's head spun. She thought she might faint.

"Let me protect you," Jeno said. "You aren't safe here."

She turned and searched his face. "Why do you want to help me?"

"Because I like you."

He lifted her in his arms and flew across the night sky up to the rock—the dimpled natural stone on the acropolis just beneath the Parthenon, where Nikita, Klaus, and Hector had sat with her two days ago. Jeno set her down on the rock beside him, where they stood totally alone. The lights of the city sparkled below, as did the stars above. The acropolis, too, was lit up like a white Christmas tree.

"It's beautiful, no?" Jeno asked.

Gertie couldn't speak. Fear and confusion had taken over her mind. Could she be having another hallucination? Maybe she had a mental illness, brought out by the trauma of leaving home against her will.

"I love my city," Jeno said. "Even if it does not love me back."

Gertie closed her eyes and opened them again, trying to wake herself up from the dream.

"This is not a dream, Gertie," he said. "And you have no mental illness. Vampires have been a part of Athens since ancient times. We are a cult of Dionysus."

"The god of mythology?"

"There's that word again. *Mythology*." He laughed. "You were so cute on the bus, correcting me about the ways of vampires."

Gertie's face flooded with heat.

"The blood in your face is beautiful," he said.

Gertie opened her mouth and closed it.

"We built a temple for Dionysus here centuries ago, and when it was moved to make way for Athena's temple, we went underground. We are cave dwellers now and can no longer tolerate the sun."

Gertie said nothing. Her body had begun to tremble and her teeth to chatter. She wanted to go home. She closed her eyes and willed herself home.

"Because we worship Dionysus, the gods allow us to stay, but they make it impossible for us to live well," he continued. "As long as we take no more than a pint of blood, we are permitted to drink."

Gertie's eyes snapped open. Was he going to drink her blood?

"No," he said. "And I only drink from the willing."

Why would anyone ever want such a thing?

"For our powers," he said, answering her silent question.

She looked at him, careful not to gaze into his eyes for long. "What are you talking about?"

"There's a reason the people of this city have come to call us tramps," he said, with a tinge of bitterness in his tone. "We have had to resort to something like prostitution in order to survive."

Gertie squeezed her eyes shut again, praying to any god who would listen.

"As long as I break no rules," he said, "the gods will not intervene."

"What gods?" she asked.

"You know the answer to that."

"You mean like Zeus? The gods of Olympus?"

"See. You do know." He grinned.

"So people give you their blood in exchange for sex?" she asked.

He laughed. "No—well, I can only speak for myself. I guess sometimes that might happen."

"Then what?"

"People give their blood in exchange for our superhuman abilities. Our bite infects them with the vampire virus for about six hours."

"Wait, are you saying…" Gertie was trying to process his words. "When you drink the blood of a human, the human does not turn into a vampire?"

"As long as we stop at a pint," Jeno explained.

"And what stops a vampire from drinking more?" she asked.

"Two things. One, it's not in our best interest to make more vampires because it would severely diminish our food supply. And two, the gods of Mount Olympus would destroy us."

"All of you?"

"The offending vampire," he said. "The gods would hunt him down, usually by sending a demigod, since the gods rarely come down to earth themselves. Only my lord Dionysus makes frequent appearances."

She studied him—his face, his mouth. She wondered if he would show her his fangs, and as soon as the thought entered her head, he flashed them.

She screamed.

He retracted them and said, "I'm sorry. I'm sorry. I didn't mean to frighten you."

"Will you take me home now?" she asked.

"Of course."

She expected him to fly her down to the metro station, but this time, when he lifted her in his arms, he flew her across the city towards downtown Athens.

"What's the address?" he asked in a husky voice.

He seemed affected by her.

He smiled at her thoughts and averted his eyes, as though from embarrassment.

He's attracted to me, she thought.

His smile widened.

She wondered if he wanted to kiss her, but she tried oh so hard to keep the thoughts in control. She failed.

He met her gaze and said, "Yes. I do want to kiss you. May I?"

He was a vampire who could take her blood by force but was, instead, seeing her home to safety. Wouldn't she be crazy to turn down the opportunity to kiss him?

"I'm much more than a vampire," he said in that husky voice. "I want you to know the real me."

She closed her eyes and leaned in as he pressed his cold lips to hers.

Chapter Ten: Hints and Warnings

When they reached the apartment building, Jeno insisted on seeing her safely inside. He set her down, and together they walked up the stairs.

She wondered why he couldn't have carried her for the rest of the way.

He grinned. "I like to be inconspicuous."

Before they reached the door, Mamá flung it open.

"Gertie?" she called down the stairs.

"It's me!" Gertie replied as she neared the landing with Jeno behind her.

"Marta!" Jeno said with surprise.

"Jeno?" Mamá covered her heart with her hand and stepped back into the doorway.

"You two know each other?" Gertie asked.

"A long time ago," Mamá muttered.

"Not so long," Jeno said with a smile.

Nikita and Klaus appeared in the doorway.

"You!" Klaus narrowed his eyes at Jeno.

"I will take my leave," Jeno said with a bow and a wink. "I hope to see you again, Gertie."

Nikita took Gertie by the hands and pulled her into the apartment as Jeno disappeared down the stairs. Klaus closed the door behind them and locked it.

"Did he bite you?" Nikita asked.

"No," Gertie said, surprised by the openness of her question.

"Babá is driving around Omonoia Square looking for you, mad with worry," Mamá said. "Klaus, can you try to call him again?"

"I'm sorry," Gertie said meekly.

"No, Gertoula," Mamá said, wrapping her arms around Gertie. "It is I who am sorry. I should not have allowed you to go alone for your walk."

As she clutched Gertie close, Mamá said a string of words in Greek, which sounded like swear words.

"I wanted you to feel comfortable and to have time to yourself," Mamá said. "But I was wrong to let you go so late. I'm sorry, koreetsi mou!"

"Why didn't you tell me about the vamps?" Gertie asked.

Mamá stepped back from the hug to meet Gertie's eyes. "I didn't want to frighten you. You understand, yes? I hoped to keep you away from the darkest secrets of Athens."

"I tried to tell you this was inevitable," Klaus said. "You can't keep that kind of secret."

"No," Mamá said, looking at Klaus. "No, Klausaki, you were right. We should have listened to you."

"Does this make you want to go home?" Nikita asked Gertie with a frown.

Gertie thought about her answer. If Nikita had asked her question a few hours ago, Gertie would have said yes. She had wanted to go home from the moment she had boarded the ferry from Venice. But now that she had met a real vampire...now she was excited and anxious to learn more.

"No," Gertie finally said. "I want to stay."

Just then, they heard the key in the door and Babá walked inside.

Mamá rushed across the room to embrace him. "I'm so glad you're safe."

Babá sighed with relief at the sight of Gertie. "No more walks alone, okay?"

Gertie nodded. As much as she hoped to see Jeno, she would never go out on the streets of Athens alone at night again.

In their bedroom, each sitting on her own bed, Nikita asked Gertie a hundred questions, and Gertie answered them all truthfully, even the part about kissing Jeno.

"I can tell he likes me," Gertie added.

"Listen to me, Gertie. He's just using you for your blood."

"Then why didn't he bite me?" Gertie asked.

"Because he knows you'll come back to him."

Gertie shook her head. "No. It's not like that. He says I'm different and interesting. He's never met anyone like me before. We have a connection."

70

"If he cares about you so much, why didn't he take you to the center of the square?" Nikita challenged.

"What are you talking about?"

"The Omonoia Square has a hexagon at its center," Nikita explained. "Vampires can't cross into it."

Gertie remembered Hector calling it the Omonoia Hexagon. "There was a bunch of homeless people there. They hollered out to me."

"They were trying to warn you," Nikita said. "To help you to safety. The beggars spend their nights in the hexagon, when they have nowhere safe to go. They stay there to avoid being seduced by the tramps."

"Seduced?" Gertie wrinkled her nose.

"Not in that way," Nikita said. "Though it does happen."

"I don't understand."

"The tramps can't take you by force," Nikita said. "But they can persuade you with their eyes and their words. They are magnetic beings, very good at attracting their prey."

Gertie shifted on the bed and leaned her back against the metal head board. "You just have to avoid eye contact."

"That's not always easy to do."

"Jeno said that humans can have a vampire's abilities for six hours after the bite," Gertie said. "Is that true?"

Nikita nodded. "Unfortunately, yes."

Gertie sat up on her knees, unable to believe Nikita's nonchalance. "How is that unfortunate? Wouldn't you love to fly, to read minds, and all of that?"

"People get addicted," Nikita said. "Once isn't enough. Then their lives fall apart, and they become beggars in the streets. Most of them die young."

"Why?"

"They forget their powers are temporary. They fall out of the sky, off buildings, fail to stop whatever object is hurling toward them. They die *every day*. And the vampires want them to die, because then they can feast on their blood without the fear of turning their victim into a vampire. They hang out at graveyards, waiting to drain the blood of the dead."

"Have you ever been bitten?"

"No. No way."

Gertie wasn't sure she believed Nikita. Who wouldn't try it, at least once, out of curiosity?

"You should talk to Hector," Nikita added. "He can tell you plenty of stories about the tramps."

"They can't help what they are," Gertie said. "They have no choice."

"Even so, they are dangerous. Promise me you'll stay away from Jeno."

Gertie said nothing. How could she make such a promise? That's all she could think about. The idea of seeing

Jeno was the only thing stopping her from begging her parents to let her come home.

Chapter Eleven: Night Visitor

The next day's plans fell through. It was the last day before school was to begin. The Angelis family had planned to take Gertie to see the Benaki Museum and some neo-classical mansions, but Babá was called in to work and needed the car. Nikita texted Hector to see if he could take them, but he had other plans. Nikita and her family members were disappointed. Gertie was relieved.

She would have an entire day to herself to read.

Should she go down to the basement to retrieve the rest of *The Vampire Chronicles*? She had to admit that, when given the choice, she still preferred to hold a paperback in her hands. Her e-reader was convenient for travelling, but the act of turning the pages and of feeling the thickness of them between her hands—being able to see how many pages were left by the feel of them rather than by a percentage sign on her screen—were in themselves a pleasurable part of her reading process. But was it important enough to risk going down to the basement?

She'd been lying on her bed posting to her favorite Goodreads groups. Nikita lay on her bed opposite Gertie listening to music through her earbuds as she read a book.

Gertie sat up with a new thought, and before thinking much about it, blurted out, "Are there vampires in the basement?"

Nikita's face fell. "What? No. Don't be ridiculous."

Gertie arched a brow, wondering how Nikita could possibly accuse her of being ridiculous after all she'd discovered about Athens.

Nikita sighed. "Not exactly."

Gertie's heart rate increased. "What's that supposed to mean?"

"I'm not allowed to talk about it."

"Why?"

Nikita pulled out the buds from her ears and jumped to her feet. "Listen, I already told you about the vamps. I'll tell you about anything else you want to know. But please, for the sake of Mamá and Babá, I beg of you not to bring up those coffins. You will crush their spirits and destroy our family worse than it already is."

Nikita left the room with her book.

Gertie sat on the bed, totally perplexed. The last thing she wanted to do was to hurt Mamá and Babá, so she decided to leave it alone for now. Yet she hoped one day she would get to the truth.

She downloaded the rest of the *Chronicles* onto her e-reader and had a reading fest all day, shut up alone in the room. Nikita had come in and out a few times, but otherwise had left Gertie alone. The whole family had seemed shaken up over her encounter with Jeno. No one wanted to talk about it. It was like they were giving themselves a day to forget about it, so they could pretend it had never happened.

But Gertie didn't want to forget.

That night, she lay in her bed thinking of Jeno and the way he had kissed her. It had been thrilling to see the effect she had had on him, to know he was attracted to her in ways that had nothing to do with blood.

When the apartment was quiet and she had nearly dozed off, she heard a voice say her name. At first, she thought it was Klaus or Bábá in the room. She sat up and turned on the lamp. Nikita snored beneath her covers, and no one else was there.

She turned off the lamp and lay back down on her pillow, only to hear the voice again. She switched on the light.

"Go to sleep," Nikita murmured. "We have school tomorrow."

Not seeing anyone else in the room, Gertie switched off the lamp and lay back down. But she did not sleep. She held her breath and listened for the voice.

"Gertie, it's me. Jeno."

What? She sat up, but did not turn on the light.

"I'm waiting for you downstairs on the street. I need to see you again. Will you meet me?"

Was she imagining his voice? She pinched herself to see if she was awake. *Ouch. Note to self: Don't pinch so hard next time.*

Laughter rang in her head—but it wasn't her own.

Without making a sound, she thought, "Are you speaking to me telepathically?"

"You really do know your vampires."

Full of excitement, she pulled back the covers and climbed out of bed.

"Where are you going?" Nikita asked without opening her eyes.

"Bathroom," Gertie lied.

She stole down the hallway to the front door, and then quietly unlocked the bolt. Turning the doorknob carefully, so as to make no noise, she inched it open a crack—enough to squeeze through, before closing it behind her. Then she crept down the stairs, praying no one would hear the creaking of the steps.

Jeno stood leaning against the railing of the steps outside the building, gazing up at the stars. It gave her a moment to study him—his tall, muscular build and long, curly hair. His skin was dark, and if it weren't for the pale moonlight and the dim street lamp, he might be invisible in his black t-shirt and denim jeans.

He looked up at her as she descended the steps and joined him on the sidewalk. The wind lifted her hair into her face, and he reached up and brushed it back for her.

"You look beautiful," he said.

"So do you."

She hadn't worn shoes. She'd come straight from bed in her white tank and shorts. She shivered with the cool breeze.

"What did you do today?" he asked. "More sightseeing?"

She shook her head. "I read about vampires."

He gave her a huge grin. "My little vampire lover."

The possessive pronoun made her heart flutter. He had called her *his*.

"Nikita said I should beware of you." Gertie was partly teasing him, but partly feeling him out. What if he did just want her for her blood? "Are you here because…"

"No. I already fed."

Feelings of jealousy surged through her as she imagined his lips on another girl.

"It was an old man who wants to feel young again," Jeno said. "We have—how shall I say—a mutually beneficial relationship."

Now her jealous feelings were replaced with those of mortification. She'd forgotten he could read her mind. Her every thought was an open book to him. The blood flooded her cheeks.

"I needed to see you again. Rarely do I have the chance to make friends."

"So you just came to talk?" she asked.

"Is that okay? Can we go for a walk? Or, we can sit here on the steps. Makes no difference to me. Are you cold?"

"I'm okay. Let's walk."

"But you have no shoes, koreetsi mou." He laughed.

"You sound like Mamá." She laughed, too.

"Perhaps you would like to fly again tonight?" he asked.

Her smile widened. "Could we?"

"Of course. You aren't afraid?"

She shook her head. "If you only knew how humdrum my life has been up to this point, Jeno." And *empty*, she wanted to add—and then she realized she had.

He leaned in and touched his lips to hers. She closed her eyes and allowed him to caress her with his mouth. She gasped.

"You are driving me wild." He grinned down at her. "Interesting, beautiful, and so very innocent. Believe me, I know humdrum. And you are no humdrum."

She beamed up at him, speechless.

He wrapped an arm around her waist. "Ready?"

"Ready."

He lifted her off the ground and into the night air. Her stomach fluttered as they flew above treetops.

"Too high?" he asked.

"Higher."

When they hovered over the skyscrapers of downtown Athens, her knees and fingers trembled with fear and excitement.

"I want to know more about you," he said.

She looked into his eyes and allowed her mind to show him her parents, her home, her private school, her one favorite teacher, the fake friends who constantly stabbed her in the back, and her lovely grandmother, who had died.

"Your grandmother was the only one who understood you, no?"

Gertie nodded, holding back tears. When her grandma had passed, Gertie had felt alone in the universe.

"You use the stories in books to fill up your heart," Jeno said.

Right again, she thought. It felt good to let someone in after years of erecting walls.

"Maybe you will make some good friends here," he said.

She smiled up at him, unable to hold back her thoughts: *I'll be leaving in one year. What's the use? How could I stay friends with people on the other side of the globe from me?*

"You don't think very highly of the power of friendship," he said.

"I guess not."

He flew quickly across the city toward the bright lights of the acropolis. They returned to the rock near the Parthenon, where they had sat together the night before.

"This is Klaus's favorite spot, too," she said.

The view was spectacular. It wasn't hard to see why so many loved to come and sit here.

"That night we met on the bus," Jeno started. "I was on my way back from saying goodbye to someone special to me. She was an old woman when she died, but she was young when we first met."

"That must be hard—watching those you care about grow old and die."

"It never gets easier."

She didn't know what to say to that.

"Can I tell you something?" he asked.

"Sure."

"I think you see your parents' lack of interest in you as—how do you say?—a reflection of *you.*"

"You don't really know enough about me to make that assumption." She didn't like the direction this conversation was going.

"Wow." Jeno shook his head and grinned.

"What?"

"You don't just have walls between yourself and *other people,*" he said. "You have walls between yourself and *your own inner soul.* What are you guarding?"

"Can we talk about something else?" She didn't expect a psychology lesson. She wanted to know about vampires—real ones.

"No, koreetsi mou, please," he said. "I thought you were different. You aren't going to ask me a hundred questions about what it is to be a vampire, are you? You already know so much. That's why I like you. I don't have to give the same boring lesson for the millionth time."

"Fair enough."

"Uh-oh," he said. "I can see the disappointment in your face." He brushed the hair from her eyes. "I'll tell you what. We each get to ask the other *one* question about a subject neither of us wishes to discuss, yes? And we both promise to answer. Okay?"

"Okay."

"Ladies first," he said.

"All right." She already knew her question. She'd been dying to ask it. He probably knew it, too. "If I let you drink my blood, what should I expect to happen?"

He covered his heart with his hand. "I don't even want to think about it."

"Why not?" She was confused.

"Because it's so hard not to think about it, and here you are asking me to."

"You said one question."

She shivered as he gazed at her throat, his longing obvious for only a moment before he grinned and said, "First, you would feel dizzy as the virus in my blood infected yours."

"Dizzy? Like sick?"

"More like drunk."

"I don't know what that feels like."

He grinned. "Oh, me. You *are* innocent. It's like falling down a rollercoaster ride. A rush."

She could relate to that feeling. "Okay so far."

"Then you would notice how you can hear the quietest sounds and see the farthest distances."

"Sounds amazing."

"When you focus in on certain people, you can even hear their thoughts."

"I'll be able to read minds?" Her mind wandered to Hector, and how she'd love to know what he was thinking.

Jeno frowned. "Is Hector your boyfriend?"

Heat flamed in her face. "No. No, I…we only just met." She was surprised by how devastated Jeno appeared.

"I'm sorry," Jeno said. "I just like you too much, I guess."

"I like you, too. Please, go on."

But his mood had shifted. His smile was gone.

"Jeno?"

"I don't want you to see me as just a vampire," he said. "I don't want the thing that lights up your face to be the consequences of my bite. I'm tired of girls using me for my powers, for the novelty of being with a vampire. When will someone be interested in Jeno? In me, as a man?"

"I'm sorry." She felt ashamed of herself, for acting like the type of person she had always abhorred: the type who used other people rather than connected with them on an intimate level. That's how all her supposed friends in New York had treated her. She came from one of the wealthiest families in America, and everyone knew it, and everyone wanted to be around her because of it. But no one seemed to care about getting to know the real Gertie.

"You don't make it easy," he said. "To get to know the real you."

"No, I guess I don't." She looked up at him. "Go ahead and ask your question."

"But I didn't finish answering yours."

"That's okay."

He held her hand. His was cold and made her shiver.

"Why do your parents ignore you?" he asked.

She hadn't expected tears to flood her eyes. She bit hard on her lip. "I suppose they're busy."

"Is that it?" He caressed her hand with his.

"They don't have to be busy," she said. "They have family money. They don't need to work. If they wanted to spend time with me, they could."

"So why don't they?"

Because they don't love me, she thought. She couldn't say it out loud.

"And why don't they love you?" he asked.

Because I'm not what they wanted. Because I'm not lovable. Because I read too much. Because I'm boring. Because, because, she broke down in tears.

He held her in his arms and said, "This is what I meant. You take it personally, but it's not your fault. Maybe they don't know how to be parents. Maybe no one showed them."

She threw her arms around his neck and cried her eyes out. He held her close and let her cry. The wind blew through their hair, the lights twinkled from both the city and the sky, and the quiet night held them.

Chapter Twelve: The American School

Gertie awoke the next morning to Mamá's voice calling through the bedroom door. She stretched and yawned. Then she bolted upright.

She couldn't recall how she had gotten back to the apartment.

Swiftly, she stole from the room to the hall bathroom and studied her reflection in the mirror. No bites on her neck. None on her wrists. The last thing she could recall was crying on Jeno's shoulder. Apparently he hadn't bitten her. So why couldn't she remember what had happened next?

Everyone in the house was excited about going to school. Gertie hadn't realized before that morning that Klaus, Nikita, and Phoebe would be attending with her, and that they would be new students, too.

"Families that host international students get preferential treatment in admissions," Klaus said at the breakfast table.

Nikita gave Klaus a dirty look.

"What?" he asked. "What did I say?"

Nikita turned to Gertie. "Mamá is hoping the new school will be better for Phoebe."

Gertie's mouth dropped open. She felt a little like the old man Jeno had mentioned—part of a mutually beneficial relationship. The Angelis family had *needed* Gertie. So much for wanting to educate a young, impressionable American about Greece.

She supposed she couldn't blame Mamá and Babá for wanting the best for their children.

A car horn blasted from the street.

"That's Hector," Mamá said. "Better hurry, glyká ta paidiá mou." She rushed around the table and gave each one of them a kiss on the cheek.

"Hector is driving us to school?" Gertie whispered to Nikita as they crossed the living area to the front door. "My mother said a bus would take me."

"Come on," she said.

This time, Klaus took the front seat beside Hector, and the three girls squeezed into the back. Hector said good morning to no one in particular. Gertie wondered if his greeting had been meant for her, too, or if he still wasn't speaking to her.

When they arrived, everyone was directed to the theater for a school-wide assembly, but they were organized by grade, so Phoebe had to go up front with the third-graders, and Hector and Klaus to the back with the seniors. Nikita and Gertie were near the back, too, with the juniors. Gertie was glad to have Nikita there with her. She hadn't expected such a large student body at an American school in Athens.

"You think Phoebe is okay by herself?" she whispered to Nikita.

Nikita frowned. "I'm praying for her."

Gertie was surprised to see that the student body was internationally diverse, and, as the first speaker addressed the students and faculty, she came to realize that, even though this was an American school, it served students from countries all over the world.

"There's a lot of people here," Gertie whispered.

"That's just because all three schools are combined, I think," Nikita replied. "The classes aren't that big."

"I get why you and your brother and sister are starting here, but why Hector?" Gertie asked.

"Mamá and Babá talked him into it," Nikita said. "He's sort of our protector."

"Protector?" This made no sense to Gertie.

"Don't ask. It's a long story."

After the school-wide assembly, the elementary and middle grades were led out of the theater, with only the high school students left behind. Nikita had been right. There were less than two hundred high school students, and only about fifty juniors. Gertie sighed with relief.

Hector, Klaus, Nikita, and Gertie were then taken on a tour, with three other new students, led by two seniors, both tall and lanky—Dimos and Joy.

They were shown the main office, the library, the cafeteria, the gymnasium, the sports fields, and the band and orchestra halls. As they stopped for Dimos to point out the

journalism room—he was the editor of the school newspaper—
Gertie heard Hector's voice softly behind her.

"So your mind could accept flying across the city with a
vampire, but not across the sea with me?"

She gasped without looking back at him. Was he
suggesting that they really had flown across the sea in the claws
of a bird?

Saying nothing in reply (what could she say?), she
followed the group back to the main office, where a counselor
gave them each a schedule. Before the group parted ways, they
all compared classes. Gertie's schedule was

Beginning Photography

English III AP

Algebra II AP

Chemistry AP

Lunch

World History AP

PE

Journalism

Gertie was glad that she and Nikita shared most of their
classes. The only periods they didn't have together were first and
last. Last period, Nikita, Klaus, and Hector had choir, while
Gertie had journalism. First period, Nikita and Klaus had art.
Gertie was caught off guard to see that Hector had photography
with her.

Nikita hugged her goodbye and followed Klaus in the opposite direction, leaving Gertie and Hector alone. The silence between them was awkward as they walked side by side down the hall.

Finally, Hector said, "What made you choose photography?"

Gertie shrugged. "I guess I like being an observer. I've never taken any pictures, though—except with my phone. I hope I won't suck at it."

Hector grinned. "I highly doubt you would suck at anything."

So he wasn't angry with her. She met his smile with her own. "Why did *you* pick it?"

"I already know how to do everything else," he said.

"Aren't *you* modest?" she teased.

The class was in progress when the two entered. The teacher welcomed them and invited them to take a seat. They sat at a back table together near a window. After the lecture, the students filled out a paper assessing their experiences with photography. Hector and Gertie laughed as they both repeatedly checked "none." Once the papers were handed back, the students were allowed to talk quietly among themselves.

"So how did you know about my flight with Jeno?" Gertie whispered, sure he would say Nikita or Klaus had told him all about her trouble in Omonoia Square.

His brows furled. "What do you mean? I was there last night. Don't you remember?"

Gertie looked back at him in shock.

The bell rang. Gertie was glad. Maybe before the end of the day, she would recall what had happened.

Chapter Thirteen: Hector

Dimos walked with Gertie from her last period to the front of the elementary school building, where Nikita, Klaus, and Hector were already waiting. Hector wore Phoebe on his back like a backpack, her legs dangling from his waist. She was smiling.

Hector looked stinking adorable.

"Good first day?" Gertie asked Phoebe.

Phoebe buried her face in Hector's back.

"I think it was," Hector answered for her. "She seems in a good mood." He bounced Phoebe and made her laugh.

It was the first time Gertie had ever heard Phoebe's voice.

"What about you, Gertie?" Nikita asked. "Good day?"

Gertie nodded. So far, none of the other students seemed like jerks.

"And you guys?" Gertie asked.

"My day was sweet," Klaus said, showing his dimples. "There's a chick in my history class already crushing on me."

Nikita punched his arm. "It's all in your head."

"I'm serious," Klaus said. "No, I mean really. I can tell."

"I believe you, man," Hector said.

They all laughed.

"What about you?" Gertie asked Nikita.

"I thought I'd know more people. I really don't know anyone."

"It won't take you long," Klaus said. "You're a social butterfly."

"Race to the car!" Hector shouted as he took off for the parking lot with Phoebe in tow.

Nikita and Klaus scrambled after Hector, who was already way ahead of them. Gertie turned to Dimos and said goodbye, and then she ran for the Mini, too.

In the car, Hector turned on the radio, and he, Klaus, and Nikita sang out loud to whatever Greek song was playing. Gertie and Phoebe exchanged glances and snickered. It was nice having Hector back to his usual happy-go-lucky self.

Once Hector pulled the Mini Cooper up in front of their apartment building, Gertie sat forward in her seat and murmured, just at Hector's ear, "We need to talk."

He climbed out and opened the door for her. "Are you free tonight?"

She briefly wondered how disappointed Jeno would be if he called to her and she was with Hector.

"Early?" she asked. "It *is* a school night, after all."

He arched a brow. "I'll pick you up in an hour. We can have dinner. I'll bring you back at nine. Sound good?"

Gertie nodded. "I'll ask Mamá."

Gertie changed into a simple straight dress that stopped a few inches above her knees. Her mother had once said that the blue brought out the blue in her eyes. Since she got few compliments from her mom, that one had stuck. She pulled her hair down from its ponytail and brushed it out. Then she added a little bit of powder and lip gloss, and she was ready to go.

Klaus whistled when she walked from the hallway bathroom into the living area.

"Hot date with Hector," he said.

"It's not a date." Gertie glanced at Nikita, where she sat on the couch.

"Then why weren't the rest of us invited?" Nikita asked.

Mamá shouted from the stove, where she was making supper, "Leave her alone, glyká ta paidiá mou. She's entitled to spend time with other people, no? Don't be so jealous."

Gertie sat on the chair by the door, waiting awkwardly. She stared at the television, but the show was in Greek.

After a few minutes, the door opened. Gertie looked up expectantly, only to see Babá walking in from work. He patted everyone's head, including Gertie's, and asked about their first day of school. Klaus and Nikita both spoke at the same time. Babá lifted Phoebe in his arms, and when Klaus and Nikita had finished, Babá asked Phoebe, "And what about you, koreetsi mou? Did *you* have a good first day?"

Phoebe nodded, wearing a big smile. Babá hugged her neck. Gertie noticed tears in his eyes.

"So maybe this was a good idea, going to the American school, no?" Babá asked Mamá.

She nodded, too. "I think so, Babáki mou."

Babá turned to Gertie. "And what did our little American think of the school? Was it as good as the one back home in New York City?"

"Better," Gertie said. "I really liked it."

Gertie couldn't recall her own father asking her once how her day at school had been.

"We should celebrate!" Babá said. "I'll bake a special cake, no?"

"Gertie has a date with Hector," Klaus said.

"It's not a date!" Gertie insisted.

"Ooo, lala," Babá teased. "A date already. And you've only been here, what, six days, no?"

"Babá, it's not a date," Gertie said again.

"It's not *Hector* she likes," Nikita said. "It's *Jeno*."

Mamá dropped a plate in the kitchen, and it shattered on the tile floor.

Klaus and Babá rushed to help clean up. Gertie and Nikita glared at one another.

The doorbell rang, but no one moved to answer it. It rang a second time, so Nikita crossed the room and opened the door.

Hector looked and smelled amazing. Everyone greeted him. Gertie expected them to embarrass her by calling it a date, but no one did—not even Nikita.

"We are going to celebrate a good first day of school with a special cake," Babá said to Hector from the kitchen. "Come back around 8:30 and celebrate with us, yes?"

"Thank you, Kyrios Angelis," Hector said. "We'll be here."

Hector walked Gertie out to the Mini and drove her away from downtown Athens.

"Where are we going?" Gertie asked after a while.

"My house. Dinner is waiting for us."

"So I'll be meeting your mom?" A ripple of nerves moved down her back.

"I hope so. She said she'll be home late from the hospital."

"Hospital?"

"She's a doctor."

"Ah."

They were quiet for a few minutes. Hector broke the silence by asking if she wanted to listen to some music. She said she'd rather talk.

"Okay," he said.

"So…" she began.

"Yes?"

"I have so many questions about last night and about the night on the ferry."

"I see." He exited the highway.

"I'm so confused. The last thing I meant to do was offend you," she added. "But what the heck happened? I dreamed of a bird."

"That wasn't a dream," Hector said as he turned right into a very nice subdivision. "The crane was my father, Hephaestus."

Gertie stopped breathing.

"So, you can believe in vampires but not in gods?" Hector asked, noticing the shock on her face.

He pulled into a long winding driveway of a beautiful two-story house.

"I'm just surprised, that's all," she finally said. "I've never met the son of a god before."

"We're all sons and daughters of gods," he said. "Some are just many more generations removed than others."

"It took me time to believe Jeno, too," she said. "You have to understand how crazy this all sounds."

"I know, especially to an American."

"Over the past couple of days, I've been wondering if I'm lying in a hospital somewhere in a coma, dreaming all of these impossible things."

"Not impossible."

He parked the Mini in a detached garage. Then, together, they walked toward the house along the beautifully landscaped lawn. When he touched the small of her back, every part of her body came to attention.

"What a beautiful home," she said once they were inside. Her eyes were drawn above the fireplace mantle to a painting of the big, white crane.

"Mamá painted that."

"Nikita's Mamá?"

"No. Mine. She's a daughter to Apollo and shares his affinity with healing and the arts."

"So your mother is a god, too?"

"Demigod, like me. Her mother was mortal."

"Was?"

"My grandmother passed a few months ago."

She laid her hand on her heart. "I'm so sorry." Then she added. "Mine did, too."

"My condolences."

"Thank you." She wondered if he had been close to his grandmother.

"Artemis was angry with her brother, Apollo. To hurt him, she tricked Hephaestus into sleeping with my mother. My mother fell in love with Hephaestus, but he never loved her in that way."

"How sad," Gertie said. "I'm sorry."

"My mother gave birth to me in my father's temple, to force him to claim me."

"And did he?"

"Once he learned of Artemis's trick," Hector said. "My mother waited in the temple for three days after she delivered me. It was hard on her. On the third night, he came to her as a crane, and he spoke to her, promising to help her to raise me."

"Do you see him often?" she asked

"Rarely. That night with you was my third time."

Gertie let that sink in. On the one hand, she was honored to have been with Hector on one of the rare occasions when he was with his father. On the other hand, what would they have done that night in the sea if Hephaestus hadn't helped them? She shuddered to think of it.

"Do Nikita and Klaus know?" she asked.

"Their whole family knows."

"Nikita said you're their protector."

"That's a story for another time."

He took her hand and led her to the dining room, where the table was set for three. The drinks and salad had been laid out.

"Let's get started," he said. "Mamá said not to wait."

"It looks delicious." She sat down. He'd gone to a lot of trouble for her—unless he did this for his mother on a regular basis. "Do you always eat like this?"

"No. Oh, hold on," he left the room and returned with a basket of rolls. "I had them in the warming drawer."

The salad greens were sprinkled with nuts and feta cheese and a delicious sweet dressing. After Gertie finished, she told him it was very good.

"Did you make this?" she asked.

"It's just chopping and assembling. Now for the main course," he said, about to get up from his chair.

"Wait," she said.

"What's wrong?"

"I've tried and tried to remember what happened last night, and I come up with nothing. The last thing I remember is crying on Jeno's shoulder. Can you please tell me when you showed up and what happened? How did I get back to my bed?"

"I heard you scream," Hector said.

Gertie's eyes widened. She had no recollection. "You must have excellent hearing."

"I could tell it was coming from the acropolis," he continued. "So I jumped in my car and drove as far as I could. Then I ran—I'm very fast, by the way. I saw Jeno fighting with his sister over you. She wanted to feed from you, but he wouldn't let her."

"So Jeno was protecting me from his sister?" she asked.

Hector frowned. "Or keeping you for himself."

"So then what?"

"I fought them off and took you home."

100

"Was anyone hurt?" she asked.

"No." The muscles near his jaw tensed.

"Did you carry me to my bed?"

He blushed. "I would have, had you needed me to. But, no, you walked."

"Why can't I remember?" she was stumped.

"Vampires have mind-controlling abilities," Hector said.

Gertie chewed on her bottom lip, wondering why Jeno would erase her memory.

"How did you end up with him last night in the first place?" Hector asked.

Gertie blushed. "He came to see me. He'd saved my life the night before."

"I heard about that," Hector said. "Though I doubt he saved your life. He just prevented you from getting bit. You would have lived."

Gertie said nothing.

"Let me get the kabobs. I hope you like them."

He left the dining room and returned in a moment with a large platter filled with food. Over a bed of white rice were laid several skewers of chunks of beef, covered in sauce. Hector moved some of the food onto a plate for Gertie. Then he served himself. Steam rose in curls from both their plates, and the aroma was tangy and appetizing.

"I'm so impressed," Gertie said as she finished her first bite. "This is wonderful. What kind of sauce is this?"

"Yogurt, tomato sauce, paprika, and cayenne pepper."

"You should work with Babá! Yum!"

"I'm glad you like it."

For the rest of the evening, they talked about school and books they had read. When they'd finished, he showed her his rooms upstairs. He had a library filled with books, and he said she could borrow any she wanted. Next door to the library was an armory with swords, knives, shields, and daggers hanging on the walls and up on shelves.

"Gifts from my father," he said.

On the other side of the armory was the music room. It was filled with stringed instruments, a baby grand piano, and drums of different shapes and sizes. He had a name for each of them.

"I like to compose my own music," he said.

"Play something for me."

"Another time," he said as his face flushed pink. "I better get you back home in time for the cake."

"I'm sorry I didn't get to meet your mom," she said as they walked back to the car.

"She will be, too," he said.

Before getting into the car, Gertie said, "Hector?"

"Yes?" He looked down at her, where she stood near the passenger's side of the Mini.

"I'm sorry I accused you of drugging me that night…"

"It's okay."

"No, listen. Please." She looked up at him. His face was so close. She couldn't resist glancing at his mouth and recalling the way he had kissed her. "If I had known it was all real, I wouldn't have kissed you like that. I..."

He took a step back.

"Because of Nikita," she added.

"Nikita?" He furled his brows.

"She likes you," Gertie said. "I wouldn't want to, you know..."

"I don't feel the same way about her," he said. "She's like a sister to me."

Gertie swallowed hard, as she returned his intense gaze. "Even so, she'd hate me. Don't you see? I have to live with her for an entire year."

"She'd get over it. It's just a school-girl crush."

"Maybe."

"But you don't want to take the chance." The muscle near his jaw flexed again.

"I just don't know."

He opened the door for her, and she climbed inside. They were quiet during the drive back to the apartment. Gertie knew she had hurt him. She liked him so much, but she just couldn't hurt Nikita. She felt like she would be betraying the whole Angelis family. They already suffered enough with the death of their little brother and with Phoebe's affliction. Tears rushed to Gertie's eyes, and, not for the first time, she wished she could go home.

Chapter Fourteen: First Bite

Although Gertie had tried not to let it show, it had been obvious to everyone that she and Hector weren't speaking to one another. Nikita's spirits seemed lifted by this, and so her good mood made up for the quiet tension between the other two as they all enjoyed Babá's special cake. Gertie was too numb inside to taste it, but she ate it anyway.

After Hector had left, and Gertie and Nikita were alone in their room with the lamp out, Nikita said, "I'm sorry about earlier."

"It's okay."

A few seconds later, Nikita asked, "So it really wasn't a date?"

"No, it wasn't."

Nikita turned on her side to face Gertie. "Can you tell me what you two talked about?"

"He told me the story of his birth—about his parents."

"Oh."

"That night on the ferry, when he jumped in, I thought he was trying to kill himself," Gertie explained. "I don't know how I thought I could help, but I jumped in after him. And then when he called to his father to help us, well, I thought it was a dream or a hallucination. I thought he had drugged me."

"It was too hard to believe," Nikita agreed.

Gertie didn't add that she had awakened without her clothes on in Hector's bed. She also didn't share what had happened last night, when she had gone with Jeno. She didn't want Nikita to know, because she was hoping Jeno would come tonight, and she didn't want her to try to talk her out of it. Gertie wanted to thank him for protecting her from his sister—because she knew that's what he was doing. She also wanted to tell him to never mess with her mind again. Erasing her memory was unacceptable, and she wanted him to explain why he had done such a thing.

Plus, she really wanted to see him.

"So Babá and Mamá seemed especially happy tonight about Phoebe," Gertie said, changing the subject.

"If you would have seen Phoebe after school before today, you'd understand why. Kids made fun of her."

"I hope they won't at the American school," Gertie said.

"Me, too. Maybe they will be more understanding and tolerant."

Gertie rolled to her side and leaned on one elbow. "Do you think she'll ever talk again?"

"I don't know. The doctors say maybe in time, but it's been three years since the fire."

"Oh."

"The fan in her room caught fire. Babá says that when he woke up from the smoke and ran into their room, Phoebe was sitting up in bed and staring at the flames. She must have been in

106

shock. He thinks that's why she won't talk now, because she couldn't talk then." Nikita's voice broke. "She might have saved Damien."

"It's not her fault."

"I know that. But she doesn't," Nikita said through tears. "At least, that's Babá's theory."

"I didn't mean to upset you."

Nikita sniffled. "I know. It's okay."

Gertie listened to Nikita's sniffles until they both fell asleep.

Sometime later, Jeno's voice awakened Gertie. He called to her in her head.

"I'm outside waiting for you," he said.

She folded back her covers and tip-toed to the front door. She let herself out quietly, and then crept down the stairs. Jeno was bathed in moonlight on the sidewalk, looking as beautiful as ever.

"Good evening," he said, as she descended the steps to the sidewalk.

"Kalo apogeyma," she said with a smile.

"Ah. So you already know Greek?"

She laughed. "Yep. The whole language."

"Eisai omorfh," he said with a grin.

In her mind, she asked what that meant.

"You look beautiful," he replied.

She blushed.

"And even more so with the blood in your cheeks," he added.

She started to ask him about last night.

"It was ugly—the fight with my sister. She got really vicious. I didn't want you to have nightmares."

"Oh." She supposed that was a good reason. "But I'm a big girl. I can handle it, okay?"

"Okay." He took her hand. "I'm sorry. Do you forgive me?"

His hand on hers sent chills up her arm. How could she not? "Yes."

He walked with her along the abandoned sidewalk. "No shoes again tonight?"

"Aren't we flying anyway?"

"As you wish. Where to?"

"Maybe not the acropolis this time. Somewhere safe, where we can be alone."

"There is no such place in Athens at night. Maybe we should go to an island I know."

"Where's that?"

"Just south of here. It's full of olive trees and sandy beaches. Some of my people used to live there in caves in the center of the island, but the human population was too small to sustain them, so they migrated elsewhere."

A shiver swept down her spine. She kept forgetting that Jeno was a real vampire who wanted blood, and his description was a frightening reminder.

"Don't be frightened, koreetsi mou," he said. "I will take good care of you."

He wrapped his arms around her waist and lifted her off the ground. They went higher and faster than they had the previous night. Her belly fluttered and her knees twitched.

"Don't let go," she said.

"Never," he whispered in her ear.

She enjoyed the sensation of his body pressed against hers. His muscular arms and hard chest exhilarated her. Her legs felt heavy as they dangled out of control beneath her, and it both comforted and excited her to be in his arms. He must have been listening to her thoughts, because she heard him sigh and felt his grip around her tighten. Then he placed the tops of his shoes beneath her feet to stop her legs from dangling.

"So thoughtful," she said to him in her mind.

He whispered in her ear, "The pleasure is all mine," and his breath sent titillating chills down her neck.

She closed her eyes and relaxed against him.

Soon they neared a small island surrounded by nothing but sea. He took her down to the sandy beach, where gentle waves lapped onto the shore. The bright moon and stars reflected on the water and in Jeno's twinkling eyes.

"It's beautiful," she said.

"One of my favorite places, for getting away. Maybe one hundred people live here—if that."

"Have you brought other girls to this place?" she asked.

He grinned. "No one as interesting and as beautiful as you."

"Nice evasive tactic." She laughed. Of course someone who had been around for centuries had brought another girl to his favorite spot. Why had she asked?

He laughed, too, as they sat together on the clean sand and gazed out at the sea. She wondered again if he wanted to drink her blood.

"I'm not hungry tonight," he said.

"The old man?"

"No." He chuckled. "It's so strange to me to discuss my feeding habits with a human. No, I can't drink from the same source each night. For each pint, I must wait one month. In the case of the old man, who wants my powers often, I take a quarter pint once a week."

"How can you tell a quarter of a pint from a whole?"

"Easily, believe me."

"I suppose you've had a lot of practice."

"More than I wish for anyone," he said softly.

He moved a strand of her hair from her eyes, and his touch brought another round of chills dancing up her body. She looked down at her toes, digging in the warm sand. She was surprised by how warm it felt, when the breeze was chilly.

"The sand absorbs the sun all day," he said. "It stays warm for many hours, but it will be cold soon."

"How old are you?" she asked. "I mean, how long have you been…"

"A vampire? I'm one of the originals."

"What does that mean?"

"Back when Dionysus first turned away from the Olympians," he explained.

"Because Hera was angry, right? Zeus fathered Dionysus with someone else."

He arched a brow. "Very good. Yes, Semele. Hera was always making trouble for Dionysus, so he left to live on his own, and he created a set of companions."

"The Maenads."

"How do you know so much?"

"I read a lot."

"My mother was one of the first Maenads. When she went wild on the wine of Dionysus, she ripped my arms from my body and drank my blood."

Gertie shuddered. "How horrible. Oh my God."

"All of the Maenads did that to their loved ones. My mother did it to my sister and father, too."

"That's how you became vampires?"

"Not quite. Zeus scolded Dionysus for his carelessness, so Dionysus repaired our bodies and turned us into the living dead. He thought his wine would sustain us, like it does the

111

Maenads, but he was wrong. We need blood to survive. If we go more than two weeks, we go into a kind of coma. That happened to my father, because he refused to drink from humans. Back then, the only way to do it was to kill them. We didn't know any other way to survive."

Gertie shuddered.

"My sister and I joined the first cult of Dionysus. Our cult built the temple on the acropolis in Athens. Over time, the gods created rules for us to abide by—rules to protect both humans and vampires. They send their demigods to enforce the rules."

Gertie thought of Hector.

Jeno shifted on the sand, stretching his legs out in front of him. "Yes, he is one of the enforcers, but the rules are more beneficial to mortals than they are to vampires. Lord Dionysus has hinted at reform, but it's never come to pass."

"What are the rules?"

"We aren't allowed to kill humans, or to take their blood without their consent."

She recalled the women in Omonoia Square.

"You can't blame us for using every technique at our disposal," he said. "We must sometimes be very persuasive. Not many humans are willing."

I am, she thought.

Jeno's eyes widened. "This isn't something to rush into."

I've given it a lot of thought, she said in her mind.

Jeno shook his head. "I don't think it's a good idea."

"Just once, to see what it's like."

He closed his eyes and took a deep breath.

"What's wrong?" she asked.

"I'm afraid you won't want to visit with me after," he said. "I really enjoy your company, and I don't want to risk not having it anymore."

"I promise that won't happen."

"I don't want you to think of me as a vampire. I want you to like me as a boy—a boy who is falling in love with a girl."

She felt the blood rush to her cheeks, and this made Jeno gasp. "Oh, me. You are so lovely in the moonlight."

"I do think of you that way, Jeno," she said, moving her face closer to his, her heart pumping wildly.

He looked at her mouth. Then he closed his eyes and kissed her.

She wrapped her arms around his neck and enjoyed the sensation of his sweet kisses. Her fingers twisted into the curls of his thick, brown hair. He moaned and kissed her harder. She pressed her body against his, and he picked her up and set her on his lap. Her hands explored his back, his shoulders, his biceps, his neck, his face. She pinched his earlobes between her fingers, and he moaned and laid her on the sand.

"You are magnificent," he whispered.

In her mind, she said, *Drink from me.*

"Are you sure, Gertie? This is what you want?" he asked.

"Yes," she breathed. "Oh, please, yes."

He kissed her lips once again, and then he slid his mouth down her throat. A sharp pain penetrated her flesh, but was numb in an instant. The star-filled sky spun in circles. In a few moments, Jeno looked down at her.

"Are you okay?" he asked gently.

She continued to gaze at the spinning stars. "Oh, my," she said, breathless.

Chapter Fifteen: Vampire Powers

"Whoa!" Gertie shouted as she lifted herself from the sandy beach into the night sky, unsteadily. She wobbled side to side, back to front, trying to maintain her balance. "The stars are so close to me. How high are we?"

"Your vision is sharper. The stars are still very far away." *You are so adorable right now.*

"I can read your mind! You better watch out, Jeno! I can hear your thoughts! You are thinking that I'm adorable! Hee-hee-hee!" She lost her balance again. The high from his bite made her light-headed. "Yikes! Am I falling?" She looked down. She was hovering just a few feet from the surface of the sea.

He laughed. "You're doing fine."

"Hey! I can walk on water!" She moved her legs, pretending to walk. "Oh! Better idea! We can go back in time!"

"Um, vampires don't time travel," Jeno corrected.

"Didn't you see *Superman*?"

Jeno looked at her blankly.

"Do vampires go to the movies?"

"Often," Jeno said. "When we have money."

"We have to fly very fast in the opposite direction of the earth's rotation. Let's see." She put her finger in her mouth and then lifted it into the air. "The earth rotates counter-clockwise. Right?"

"How do you know such a thing?"

115

"I told you. I read a lot." She put her hands on her hips. "This means we have to fly clockwise if we're going to stop the earth and make it turn the other way."

"Stop the earth?" He busted out laughing. "What are you talking about?"

"Come with me!" She soared up into the dark night. It was exhilarating and scary. *Don't look down*, she told herself.

"We can't stop the earth, Gertie." He caught up to her. "Don't you think airplanes would have done that if it were possible?"

"That's right!" she stopped in mid-air. "We have to break through the earth's atmosphere."

Jeno stopped an instant later but was going so fast that he had to backtrack several feet to get back to her. "Break through the atmosphere? How would we survive?"

"That's right. No oxygen. Wait, do vampires breathe?" she asked.

"Of course we do. How else would we oxygenate the blood we drink?"

"But…"

"Our bodies would deteriorate without oxygen."

"Oh."

"And, besides, from what I've read…"

"Wait," she said. "You read? Vampires read? Get out!" She planted both palms on his chest and shoved. He didn't move but a few inches.

He rolled his eyes. "I'm not just a vampire. And yes, we have a lot of time on our hands. We go to the movies. Some of us read. In the dark. With night vision. Sheesh!"

"What books have you read?" she asked. "Do you have a favorite?"

"I'm a huge fan of historical fiction," he said.

"I love historical fiction! I love learning about the past! And our textbooks at school can be so dry!"

"I think I enjoy it for different reasons than you." He winked. "I like laughing at all the parts they get wrong—even the historians get most of it wrong. Sometimes it seems on purpose, in my opinion. They want to rewrite history."

"That's why we should go back in time! Then I could see the past for what it really was!"

"Surely you know what happens when an object breaks through the earth's atmosphere," he said.

"Oh, yeah. It burns," she said, deflated. "Then how did Superman do it?"

"Isn't he a cartoon character?"

"Comic book," she said.

"So no time-travelling, my little vampire lover. Okay?"

"Okay." She looked at him—really looked at him—for the first time since he had bitten her and realized she had x-ray vision. She could see though his clothes.

He lifted his chin and guffawed.

She broke out in hysterical laughter, too, as heat rushed to her face.

"Do you like what you see?" he asked.

If she could see him, he could see her, too. Her cheeks burned with blood, as she grew quiet. He laughed even harder.

"Don't be shy," he said. "On this very beach is a nudist colony. Many of these islands have them. It's natural, especially in the tropical heat."

She looked again over his body through his clothes.

"Take as much time you need," he said in a cocky tone, posing for her.

She punched his arm.

"Ow! Don't forget, you have super strength, too. And that hurt." He pretended to pout, looking incredibly sexy.

She giggled and rubbed his arm, enjoying the feel of his firm bicep beneath her fingertips. "Oops. Sorry."

He smiled, leaned in, and kissed her.

They took off flying over the sea back toward Athens. Jeno let her take the lead, but he directed from behind, his arm around her waist, his palm against her mid-drift, his front snug against her back. He pointed out landmarks down below as they passed them. He flew with his face right beside her own, speaking into her ear. It was romantic and thrilling to have him close and to see so far. With her night and x-ray vision, she could see the minute details of the ruins and architectural gems he named. Gertie had never imagined that she'd have a tour of Greece in quite this way.

As they neared Athens, Gertie imagined swinging from building to building, like Spiderman.

"We can do whatever you'd like," Jeno said in response to her thought. "I'll take care of you."

They descended to the top of a skyscraper and landed on the roof. The wind was brisk, and few cars were out on the streets below.

"Won't people see us?" she asked.

"We can make ourselves invisible." He disappeared.

"Jeno?" Her heart skipped a beat. Had he left there alone?

"Right here." She felt his hand on her shoulder. "You can do this, too. Just take a deep breath, and imagine pulling all of your outer energy into your core."

She took a deep breath. "Like this?"

He laughed. "No, no. You're pushing your energy outward. But you look cute standing there with wide eyes, imaging yourself invisible."

She punched his arm.

"Watch it," he said, laughing.

"How do I do it, then? How do I pull it all in?"

"Invisibility is a defense mechanism. Imagine you're being attacked, and you're withdrawing into a shell, like a turtle."

She did as he said. She tried this a few times, punching him as he laughed.

At last, she could no longer see herself, but her clothes were still visible.

"There you go," he said. "Good."

"We can't even see our own bodies? I would think…"

"No, you can't, because it has to do with the reflective power of your cells. You can't reflect light. You have to push the energy outward again to hit the light and be visible, even to your own eyes."

She pushed her energy out, and her body appeared again. Then she withdrew, like a turtle in its shell, and she vanished.

"Incredible!" she cried. "But why can I still see my clothes?"

"You can't change the reflective cells in clothing."

"Then why can't I see yours?"

"Because I'm not wearing clothes. I created an illusion."

"So you go around nude all the time?"

"Pretty much."

"Is that true of all vampires?"

"Probably, but I don't know."

Gertie blushed at the thought of being with Jeno, while he wore no clothes. It was difficult to get past that idea.

"So I have to remove mine?" she asked.

"If you don't want to be noticed."

She supposed her clothes provided no protection from his x-ray vision anyway. She took off her clothes and piled them in a heap on the rooftop.

Jeno chuckled, felt for her hand, and said, "Ready to building-hop?"

"Absolutely!"

"Hold on!"

They both lifted up into the air and hopped onto the roof of a neighboring skyscraper. She screamed with delight as her stomach lurched into her chest and her head spun. It was like riding a roller coaster. A bit different from flying, hopping was the use of their leg muscles to fling themselves to the next building. Without being able to see her own feet, the landings were a bit awkward until she got used to them.

They hopped from rooftop to rooftop for a good half hour, laughing like children. Then Jeno stopped and became visible again.

"What's wrong?" she asked. "Too tired to go on?"

He grinned. "I just wanted to see you again." He handed over her clothes. "Here, if these make you feel better."

She climbed into them because, yes, they did make her feel better. When she turned her energy outward, her body reappeared.

"Fascinating," she said.

"Yes, you are."

The waning moon shone down on them, and the wind lifted their hair around their faces. He took her in his arms for another sweet kiss. She loved the feeling of being enveloped in his arms. She looked up at his adorable face as he gazed down at her with his dark, round eyes. His thick, curly hair blew into her face. His thick lips spread into a smile that melted her heart. She lifted her face up to his for another kiss, unable to believe that, of all the girls Jeno could choose to spend his time with, he'd chosen her.

When he wrapped his arms around her and held her in a tight embrace, she rested her cheek on his broad shoulder and sighed. The city below came into sharp view. The sight of a vampire was amazing. She couldn't stop looking at things far away, just because she could see them. She caught a glance of Hector's subdivision in the distance, and her thoughts were suddenly of him and the evening they had spent together. She tried to get him out of her mind, not wanting to hurt Jeno; but, as she pictured Hector in his house, his thoughts came rushing to her mind.

And Hector's thoughts were of her:

I can't stop thinking about that night and the way she touched me. Father, please help me to find a way to either forget that night or to win her love.

Jeno took in a sharp breath.

When she gazed up at him, he wore the saddest expression she'd ever seen.

"He's in love with you," he said.

"But I'm not in love with him," she insisted.

"You're lying to yourself," he said, lifting up from the rooftop.

"Where are you going? Please, don't leave me."

"I only go where I'm wanted."

She flew after him, over the lights of the city. "It's you I want. I swear." She hadn't known either boy long enough to be in love, but she didn't want Jeno to leave. She was falling for him—hard. She supposed she had feelings for Hector, too.

"You forget I can read your mind."

She caught up to him. "Why can't I read yours?" She was getting nothing, as though a wall had been put up around him.

"I've blocked you. Now go."

"Why are you doing this?" She grabbed his arm. "I was having such a good time with you."

"I've been burned too many times—more times than I would wish for anyone."

He pulled her close, pressed his lips to hers, and then broke away from her grip and flew off before she could blink.

She was left alone hovering in the night sky above Athens.

Chapter Sixteen: Tramp Stamp

Mamá's voice called through the bedroom door and stirred Gertie from her sleep. She opened her eyes to see Nikita sit up and stretch her arms.

"I wonder if this is going to be another good day for Phoebe," Nikita said.

"I hope so."

A massive headache pounded in her head as Gertie pulled back her covers and swung her feet onto the floor. Memories of the previous night flooded her—being with Jeno, using his powers, and then being left behind. Not knowing what else to do, she'd flown home and laid in bed, listening to people's dreams. Like her, Hector hadn't been sleeping. All night long, he had thought of her and how sad he was that she was unwilling to risk her relationship with Nikita to give him a chance.

"How did your feet get so dirty?" Nikita asked.

"What?" Gertie glanced down and noticed the dirt crusted around her toes. She crossed one leg over the other to inspect the bottom of one foot, only to find it horrendously black. "Maybe I walked in my sleep?"

"Oh my God!" Nikita cried, gawking at Gertie.

"What's the matter? Why are you looking at me like that?"

"Tramp stamp," Nikita muttered, pointing at Gertie's neck. "You were bitten by a tramp!"

Gertie's hand flew to the bite mark on her neck as blood rushed to her cheeks. "Don't tell anyone. Please?"

"How could you do it? After all I told you?"

"I had to try it once." Gertie stood from the bed. "Don't tell me you've never tried it, just to see what it's like."

Nikita shook her head. "No way."

"But, Nikita, it was incredible!" Gertie's head pounded as she moved around, but she ignored it as best as she could. "I flew all over Greece, hopped on buildings, went invisible, saw the smallest and furthest things, read minds—it was amazing!"

"Read minds? Did you read *my* mind?"

"You were asleep, so no, but I did get a peek at your dream."

Nikita stood up and crossed the room. "Don't do that ever again."

"I don't plan to," Gertie insisted. "I just wanted to see what it was like."

"That's what everyone thinks, and before you know it, they can't get enough."

"It won't happen to me."

Nikita left the room and went down the hall to the bathroom. Mamá's voice called to them to come for breakfast. Gertie dressed as quickly as possible, tired from her lack of sleep and from the pounding in her head.

When Nikita returned to their room, she pulled a scarf from one of her drawers and gave it to Gertie. "Wear this. Don't let anyone see your stamp—especially Mamá and Babá. It would break their hearts."

Gertie wrapped the silk floral scarf around her neck. "Thanks."

"Not everyone knows the truth about the tramps," Nikita added. "Even many Greeks are ignorant. Most of those who know live in the inner city, like us. And those who know of them will despise you if they see your stamp."

"Why?"

"They will think of you as a traitor to the human race. Most people hope the tramps will die off."

But according to Jeno, the vampires didn't die; they went into a kind of coma. Gertie wondered if Nikita knew that.

Although the day started off poorly for Gertie—including the somewhat awkward silence in the car ride to school—the day picked up when she discovered that her academic level was above most of the other students at the school. She scored high grades on her assignments and received a compliment from her English teacher after answering a question in class about the purpose of literature.

Gertie had said, "It helps us to live beyond the limitations of our own experiences."

"Quite insightful, Gertie," the teacher had said. "Excellent answer."

In journalism, Dimos and his friends were also chummy with her, and they were *seniors*. These people knew nothing of her family's money, so the fact that they were nice to her was a boost to Gertie's ego. By the end of the day, she felt much better than she had that morning.

Adding to her good spirits was the discovery that Phoebe had made a friend. A little girl stood beside Phoebe in front of the elementary school, where they had met for their ride home with Hector. The other little girl was teaching Phoebe signs, and Phoebe was trying them. She learned "yes," "no," "thank you," "you're welcome," and "goodbye." All four teens were so excited for Phoebe, that the car was once again full of laughter and song during the drive home. Even Gertie sang along when she could figure out the words.

When Hector pulled up in front of their apartment building, Nikita begged him to come up and visit before going home. Klaus talked him into doing homework together. So Hector parked and they all went up. Nikita was beaming.

Mamá was waiting for them in the kitchen with homemade pastries and fresh fruit, so they gathered around the table and told her about their day. Phoebe showed her the sign language she'd learned from her new friend. Mamá broke down in tears and showered Phoebe with wet kisses.

Once they had finished Mamá's pastries, they took out their books and started their homework. Gertie worked through her math quickly, and then took her time reading her history assignment. She recalled her conversation with Jeno and wondered how much of the information in her book was wrong, but thinking of him soon made her sad. She really hoped he would come to her again tonight, even though she was so sleepy. She would no doubt be going to bed right after dinner, if not before.

When Babá walked in from work, the semi-silent room got boisterous as everyone relayed the events of their day to him. Phoebe demonstrated the signs she had learned, and like Mamá, Babá was quickly teary-eyed. He rushed around the room, kissing the tops of everyone's heads, including Hector's. Then he announced he would bake another special cake to celebrate the *second* day of school.

"Is Hector invited to stay?" Nikita asked.

"Of course, koreetsi mou!" Babá replied. "Now let me tell you about *my* day! A funny, old woman came into the café, and this is what she said."

Just as Gertie was wondering how they managed to stay thin with all the food Mamá and Babá continually put in front of them, Babá pulled the scarf from Gertie's neck and wrapped it around his head, speaking in an old lady's voice. Before he had finished his story, Mamá gasped and gawked at Gertie.

Gertie couldn't believe she had already forgotten about the mark. Her hand rushed to her neck; but, it was too late. Everyone had already seen it.

She was glad she no longer had the ability to read minds, because the looks on the faces of everyone around the table told her more than she wanted to know. Everyone there was shocked, fearful, and disgusted.

"Perhaps Hector should go," Mamá said.

"But he can help her," Nikita insisted.

Hector stood up. "No, I think your mother is right. I better go."

Gertie closed her eyes and swallowed hard as Hector left the apartment. She doubted he would ever speak to her again.

Babá handed Gertie the scarf. "Put this back on, please. The mark is offensive."

Gertie noticed Mamá's hands rush to her own throat, as if she feared the bite was contagious.

Mamá touched her husband's shoulder. "I'll have a talk with her, no? Come on, Gertie."

Gertie put the scarf back on and followed Mamá down the stairs and out of the apartment building. They sat side by side on the outside steps. Rush hour traffic jammed the street, and lines of people passed along the sidewalk. The noise of the traffic was loud enough to prevent the passersby from overhearing what Mamá had to say.

"Tell me why you did this, Gertoula."

"Curiosity."

"Don't the Americans have a saying about curiosity?"

Gertie nodded. "It killed the cat."

"If you do this terrible thing again, it could kill you."
Mamá took Gertie's hands. "Humans die all the time from the
misuse of the power they receive from the bite. And the tramps
don't always stop like they are supposed to. You could die—or
worse, you could become one of those leeches yourself. Don't
you see? It's too dangerous to have dealings with them. It's best
to avoid them."

"I won't do it again, Mamá. I promise."

"Thank you, Gertie." Mamá kissed her cheek. "You are
a good girl. Your parents would never forgive me if anything
happened to you while you're in my care."

"I doubt that," Gertie muttered.

Mamá jolted her head back. "Gertrude! How can you say
such a thing?"

Gertie shrugged. "They are very different from you and
Babá."

"Nonsense. I know your mother. She would kill me if
anything happened to her little girl."

It was Gertie's turn to throw her head back in surprise.
"How do you know my mother?"

"Dhen katalaveno, I mean, I don't understand why she
wouldn't have told you." Mamá pulled her knees in close and
hugged them. "We were friends, the year she came to Greece."

Gertie didn't know what to say. She couldn't even
picture it. She'd never met two women more different. "My
mother and I don't talk very often."

Mamá met Gertie's gaze. "I'm sorry to hear that. I hope you know you can talk to me any time."

"Thank you." Gertie gave her a half smile.

"Will you promise me another thing?"

Gertie nodded.

"Stay away from Jeno."

Gertie's mouth dropped open. "But he's my friend."

"That's not possible."

"He only bit me because I begged him to. He didn't want to do it."

Mamá shook her head. "No, koureetsi mou. He only told you those things."

"We *really are* friends. We have a lot in common."

"I'm not saying Jeno isn't a kind person, or that he is incapable of love." Mamá cupped Gertie's face. "But he cannot be a friend to anyone. No matter how nice he seems, it is in his nature to use people. His need for blood will always be more important to him than your friendship."

Gertie bit her lip. Mamá did not know what Jeno had said to Gertie—about wanting to be seen as something other than a vampire. She didn't see firsthand how hesitant Jeno was to bite her, and how he had only done it because she had pleaded with him. Maybe Mamá had bitter feelings toward Jeno because of something that happened between them in the past.

"How do you know Jeno?" Gertie asked.

Mamá dropped her hands and bowed her head, as though she were studying the ants on the concrete steps. "It was a long time ago."

"Did my mother know him, too?" A sudden chill crept up Gertie's back.

"No. Well, she knew of him. Her boyfriend didn't approve of her making his acquaintance."

"Boyfriend?" Gertie's back straightened. "You mean my father?"

"No. I never met your father. Your mother was in love with a boy here in Athens. But that was so long ago."

Gertie linked her hands together, as though she were about to pray. "Please tell me all about it!"

Mamá grinned. "That is your mother's story to tell, not mine. You should ask her, no?"

Gertie wondered if her mother had any photographs. She would definitely ask when she returned home.

"Listen to me. This is important. And you must keep this a secret for me."

"I promise." Gertie studied Mamá's face. Even up close she seemed young and beautiful.

"I was once in love with Jeno, when I was your age."

Gertie sucked in air and stared back blankly.

"I'm telling you the truth," Mamá added.

"So you knew him well."

"Yes. Very well."

"Did you let him bite you?"

"Not for many months. It was like you said—he didn't want to. He couldn't help that he was a vampire, and he didn't want to be that way with me. He tried to keep the two lives separate, but it was impossible."

"Why?"

"Vampires use tactics to lure humans into offering their blood. Seduction is one such tactic. Too many times, I saw him use sweet words and affectionate phrases with other girls, who were his prey."

Gertie shuddered.

"He was such a good liar. It made it difficult for me to believe him when he told me he loved me."

"Why did you let him bite you, then?" Gertie asked.

"I thought I could be enough for him. I thought he could live on my blood, and then he wouldn't have to lure the other girls into his arms."

"He needed more than you alone could give him," Gertie said.

Mamá nodded. "It was hard to leave him, but I had no choice. A life with him was no kind of life. Fortunately, I met and fell in love with Babá soon after. By the time I met your mother, Jeno was out of my life."

"How long ago was it that you saw him last?" Gertie asked. "Were you in high school?"

"Three years ago—briefly." Mamá gazed across the street with a blank look on her face. She moved the pendant on her necklace back and forth on its chain, as though she were in a trance. "I needed his help."

"With what?"

Mamá continued to gaze blankly across the street, fiddling with her necklace.

"Mamá?" Gertie asked.

"Huh?" Mamá looked at her. "Oh, sorry. What did you say?"

"Why did you need Jeno's help?"

Mamá climbed to her feet. "It's a long story. Now, let's go inside."

Chapter Seventeen: Silent Treatment

Gertie avoided the eyes of everyone at the table when she and Mamá returned from their talk. Tired and embarrassed, she went straight to her room and got ready for bed. As she lay there, alone, she allowed herself to cry. She'd been in Greece for less than two weeks, and she'd already managed to make everyone hate her. She closed her eyes and hoped Jeno would come for her. She really needed a friend right now, and, even though she believed most of what Mamá had said, she refused to accept the idea that Jeno could never be a true friend.

She also wondered what Mamá was keeping from her about the help she had needed from Jeno three years ago. Gertie wondered if it had something to do with the fire that had killed Damien.

Mamá's voice called through the door, pulling Gertie from a strange dream.

"Are you okay?" Nikita asked. "You were crying in your sleep."

"I was?" Gertie wiped her eyes to find them still wet. She couldn't believe it was already morning. She'd slept through the night, without waking once. That meant Jeno hadn't come for her. "Yeah. I'm all right."

Nikita got up and rummaged through a drawer, pulling out scarves. "You can borrow any of these you want."

"Thanks. Does this mean you're not mad at me?"

"I'm not one to hold a grudge. Let's just forget about it and put it behind us, okay?"

Gertie nodded, one of the knots in her stomach releasing a little. She took a deep breath.

"The shower's free, girls!" Mamá called. "One of you jump in!"

"You can go first," Nikita said.

Although Hector never met her eyes or spoke a word to her, the car ride to school was not quiet and solemn, thanks to Nikita. She chatted away about a choir performance they were preparing for the fall festival. She convinced the boys to practice with her on the way. The harmonizing voices took the edge off of Gertie's anxiety.

Photography class got real awkward real fast when the teacher paired Gertie and Hector together for a class project. They were told to go outside on campus with their equipment and shoot portraits of one another. The background needed to contrast in some way with the person in the foreground. Those were their only guidelines.

Hector and Gertie walked around the campus, aimlessly, it seemed, in silence. There were so many things Gertie wanted to say to him, like, "Please don't hate me," "I didn't mean to hurt anyone," "Jeno is not what you think," and "I need your friendship." She also wanted to say that if Nikita weren't so in

136

love with him, she would allow herself to think differently about him, but then she thought better of it. Better to stay silent on that subject.

Eventually they came to the front of the school, to the fountain. The fountain was circular and layered, like a wedding cake. Water poured from the top bowl into three others—each larger in diameter than the one above it. The water eventually pooled into a fifteen-foot-wide reservoir. The bottom of the reservoir was littered with coins.

"Stand there," Hector pointed to the front of the fountain.

Gertie did as he said. He aimed his camera and took a few shots. She didn't smile or pose or anything—just stood there.

"Now where do you want me?" he asked.

She glanced around, at a loss. Did it matter?

He took a few steps toward her. "Aren't you curious as to why I chose this spot?"

"I didn't realize you had put any thought behind it."

"We were told to choose a background that contrasted with the foreground, right?"

She nodded.

"Well this fountain is the opposite of you."

She crossed her arms and waited for him to explain.

"The water flows freely, whereas you hold everything in."

"Now wait a minute." She pointed a finger at him. *"You're* the one who isn't speaking to *me.*"

"What? I said good morning, and you said nothing."

"You weren't talking to *me.*"

"Aha." He stepped closer. "You *assumed* I wasn't talking to you."

"You're the one who left when you found out about the bite."

"Because I knew how upset the Angelis family was. I didn't want to be in the way."

"You were angry with me, too. You all were. You all hate me now."

"I was jealous." He stepped so close to her, their arms touched. "And I don't hate you. Neither do they."

Tears rushed to her eyes. "I was just curious. And I'm not really sorry I did it."

He took a step back. "Even though it upset everyone?"

She slapped her free hand against her thigh. "I didn't mean to upset them. Of course I don't like to see them hurt. But I'd do it again. Hector, I could *fly.* I could leap from one building to another. I made myself *invisible.*" She swallowed hard, averting her eyes. "And I could hear people's thoughts."

"Whose thoughts?"

"Anyone's. I didn't just hear a whole bunch of random thinking. I had to focus on specific people. Most people were asleep, so I just saw their dreams."

"Most? That means there were others whose thoughts you heard."

She shrugged. "Random people."

"You focused on random people?"

Heat rushed to her face.

He shook his head and walked away.

She caught up to him. "Doesn't it make you feel good that I wanted to know what you were thinking? Doesn't it show that I..."

He stopped and faced her. "That you what?"

Dare she say, "Care about you"? She held her tongue.

"Didn't it occur to you that it's wrong to violate people's minds like that?" he asked. "You can't just pop into people's heads. It's worse than stealing. Don't you get that?"

"Oh," she said. "I didn't think of it that way. I'm sorry."

"But you already said you would do it all over again. How can you be sorry?"

"Reading minds. That's the part I regret."

"There's a reason mortals can't fly, or leap from buildings, or go invisible," he added.

"Why?"

"Because it's dangerous. The human body wasn't made for those things. Do you know how many people die because they get addicted to the powers of the tramps? They get to the point where they can't stop."

"I already got this lecture."

"But still, you would do it again."

"Just once."

He sighed. "The bell's about to ring. Are you going to take a photo of me, or not?"

Around the corner of the building, the lawn was in shadows.

"Over there," she said. "In the shade."

He stood by the side of the building. He crossed his arms and glared back at the camera while she aimed and shot. She only needed one.

As they walked back to their classroom, she said, "I shot you in the shade because you are the opposite of darkness. You bring light to everyone around you."

She didn't look at him, and he didn't look at her, but she could tell her words had affected him.

After two weeks of this same awkward tension between her and Hector—not to mention between her and Mamá and Babá—Gertie found herself missing Jeno. Each night, she hoped he would come; each morning, she woke up, disappointed.

One night, she lay in bed, wondering if she should go looking for him. She had promised Mamá and Babá that she would not walk the streets of Athens alone at night, but that was before Nikita had explained about the Omonoia Hexagon. Now that she knew how to protect herself, things were different, weren't they? Plus, it wasn't like Mamá and Babá were always completely honest with her. She lay there for over an hour, weighing the pros and cons. One minute, she was sure she would go; the next, she was sure she would not.

She decided to go for it. She had already lost their love and respect anyway, so, even if they *did* find out, she had nothing more to lose. She had everything to gain.

She scooped up Nikita's flip flops and tip-toed across the apartment, letting herself out the front door. Once she was down on the street, she slipped on the shoes and headed toward Omonoia Square.

Gertie avoided eye contact with the people she passed on the sidewalk, but she looked over them, hoping to find Jeno. When she reached the square and still had not found him, she wondered if it would do any good to ask around. The idea of approaching the tramps got her heart beating crazily. Those around her must have noticed, because they looked her way with interest. Frightened, she ran to the center of the hexagon where a few other people had already gathered.

The vampires couldn't take her by force, even on the outside of the hexagon, but, out there, they could use mind control.

The night air was chilly, and she wore nothing but her tank top and shorts. She rubbed her arms to create heat and stepped side to side as she watched the people in and around the square.

When a man passed by, she took a chance that he might be a tramp. There was something in his confidence and in his gaze, especially the way he eyed the people huddled together in the center of the square. The biggest tell was his extraordinary good looks.

"Have you seen Jeno?" she asked him.

His brows shot up with surprise, disappearing behind his long, dark hair. "Why do you ask?"

"I need to talk to him," she said, avoiding his dark eyes.

"Then call him." The man was tall and thin and wearing a business suit, but he had long, untidy hair, and he had dirty hands. He continued on his way.

"I don't have his number."

The man stopped, turned to face her, and guffawed. Then he said, "Come here and I will take you to him."

Gertie cocked her head to one side, considering it.

"Don't go," said an older man standing next to her, who was toothless and probably homeless. "He's a vreak."

"Butt out, old man," the tramp said. Then to Gertie, he asked, "Are you coming?"

Gertie shook her head. "No, thank you." She didn't trust him.

The tramp asked, "Why do you need to talk to Jeno? Maybe I can give him a message."

Gertie didn't see any harm in that. "He's my friend. I want him to know that. I want to see him."

"Thee moy," the homeless man beside her said.

The tramp in the suit stepped toward her and dipped his head. "I shall give him your message."

When the tramp left, Gertie wished she had gone with him. All she could do now was stand around and wait.

Then it occurred to her why the tramp had laughed at her when she'd said she didn't have Jeno's phone number. He hadn't meant for her to call him by phone. He had meant for her to call out for him.

Cupping her hands around her mouth, she shouted, "Jeno!"

People looked in her direction, but then kept walking.

After a few minutes, she called to him again. "Jeno!"

Maybe he couldn't hear her as long as she was in the center of the square. With her heart pumping madly, she took several steps, unsure where the hexagon began and ended. She studied the tiles and soon saw the pattern.

"Don't go out there," the old, toothless man warned her.

She stepped over the line and shouted again, "Jeno!"

Several tramps walked in her direction.

"Mporo na sas voythYso?" one of them asked. "Can I help you?"

Another soon appeared a few inches away. It was one of the women from the other night. "Elate mazy mou."

"I'm looking for Jeno," Gertie said.

143

"Elate mazy mou," the woman repeated, gazing into Gertie's eyes.

Gertie broke eye contact.

"Leave her alone," a voice hissed as a hand reached for hers.

Gertie looked up, expecting to see Jeno, but it was the tramp in the business suit.

"Come with me," he said. "I will take you to your friend."

They broke free of the crowd that had gathered around her, as some of the other tramps called after them.

"Come back!" the old, toothless man in the center of the square shouted.

The vampire put his hand around her waist and lifted her into the night sky.

"Alexander," he said, when she had wondered what his name was.

"Where are we going?" She felt dizzy and frightened. She still didn't trust him.

"To a rooftop, where Jeno likes to hang out."

Gertie thought of Jeno's real favorite spot—the island of olive trees and sandy beaches.

"Ah. Good idea." Alexander shifted direction and accelerated in speed.

Gertie's stomach lurched. She had a bad feeling.

When they landed on the beach, Jeno was nowhere in sight. Before she could cry out for her vampire friend, Alexander clutched her face with his grimy paws and pressed his foul mouth to hers.

She squirmed and shoved against him, saying, "Stop! What are you doing?"

"I know you want this," Alexander said smoothly, as he held her flailing body against his.

"No I don't!" she screamed.

"Your lips say one thing, but your mind says another."

He pushed her down on the sand, straddled her waist, and stretched open his mouth. The moonlight glinted against his long, sharp fangs.

Chapter Eighteen: Second Bite

Alexander's fangs sank into her neck. Unlike Jeno, who took a small taste of her blood, the tramp in the suit sucked and sucked for what seemed like an eternity.

Gertie's head spun. She closed her eyes as the high from the bite made her feel light and airy. When she opened them, Alexander was gone.

She sat up, her head reeling. After blinking several times, the crescent moon finally came into view. Her sharp eyes could make out its craters and the part of it that was in shadows. The stars, too, were distinct bodies rather than their usual blurs of light. She climbed to her feet, brushed off sand, and tried to get her bearings. Which way was home?

Without Jeno to guide her, she was afraid to take off across the sea. She recalled the last time she had fallen into its icy swells, terrified of the predators swimming below the surface.

"Jeno!" she shouted desperately into the quiet night.

When he didn't appear, she tried to hone in on his thoughts, but she couldn't focus on him without knowledge of his location. Then she tried Hector. She found him asleep and dreaming. Remembering what he had said—that mind-reading was worse than stealing—she pulled back to her solitary thoughts.

She had no choice but to fly on her own.

With her arms stretched out, she pushed off the ground and into the air. Like the last time, she wobbled as she tried to maintain her balance. First, she flew a few feet above the sand, in case she fell. Once she had the hang of it, she soared higher. Exhilaration surged through her. She'd forgotten how thrilling this was. She experimented with a forward flip, her unintentional squeal shattering the quiet night. When that was successful, she tried it backwards. She flew forwards, backwards, and sideways. She glided slowly and then shot across the sky.

Confident now, she flung herself out, above the sea, in the direction she hoped would lead her to Athens.

From this higher vantage point, she could see the lights along the southern shores of Greece. The buildings soon came into view. Her eagle eyes fell upon the Parthenon, and she went for it, full speed ahead.

Once she landed on the acropolis, alone, beneath the night sky, she cried out, "Jeno!" She imagined him in the secret caves below her. She was surprised when she heard his thoughts, and even more surprised when he reacted to her presence in his head.

Who did this to you? He asked telepathically.

Please come out and talk to me.

That is not a good idea. Go home, koureetsi mou.

Please?

I haven't fed for many days. I can't take the temptation.

Why haven't you fed?

He didn't answer her directly, but she saw his thoughts. He'd been depressed since they had last parted. He'd wanted badly to see her, but he'd been too afraid.

Jeno, please. To herself, she thought, "How can a vampire be afraid of *me*?"

Not you. His mind revealed that he was afraid of a broken heart. *It's happened too many times in my long life. I try to avoid it.*

Refusing to take no for an answer, she scanned the sides of the acropolis for the entrances into the caves. She found one, boarded up, and, supposing vampires were able to walk through walls, she flung herself against the wood.

The boards crashed to the ground, and she fell on them, but it didn't hurt.

I guess that's not how a vampire does it, she thought as she climbed to her feet and dusted her knees.

Get out of here! It's too dangerous! Jeno warned.

With her night vision, Gertie charged through the narrow, winding tunnel. A vampire came out of nowhere and bit her wrist before she knocked it away. Another bit her leg. She kicked it. Hissing and screeching sounds echoed throughout the narrow passageway.

Then Jeno appeared before her. "Get out! Are you crazy? You're fair game in here."

He took her hand and led her out where the stars and moon once again shone down on her.

"Thee moy," he said. "You've lost so much blood. Perhaps too much. Who did this?"

The name of the one responsible popped into her mind: *Alexander.*

"I'm going to kill him," Jeno said.

"I feel fine."

"You do now, but when the vampire virus is out of your system and your powers have faded away, you will feel faint— maybe even sick."

She heard his thoughts. He longed for her blood and was fighting the temptation to taste it.

"Go ahead and take some," she said. "Please. You're starving."

"You've already lost too much. I can tell in your color." He punched his fist into his hand. "I'm going to kill Alexander."

"You're going to go into a coma if you don't feed," she reminded him.

He sat on a nearby rock. "Maybe it's for the best."

"How can you say that?" She sat beside him.

He didn't have to explain. His thoughts were an open book to her:

The night I met you on the bus, I was returning home, after saying goodbye to someone I loved. I met her thirty years ago. When she died, I wanted to die, too. But on the bus ride home, I met you, and I realized it was possible to become interested in another person.

149

When I got off the bus, I knew you and I would meet again.

But I cannot compete with Hector.

After I last left you, I walked the streets of Athens, hoping to meet another friend to take my mind off the one I lost—the woman I had to bury.

"And did that work?" she asked.

No. All I've thought about is you.

"And all I've thought about is you," she said, leaning closer. "Why do you think I've come here?"

"You like the power."

"I like *you*." She took his hand. "Please take a little sip—just to keep from going into a coma. I can handle it. I promise."

He licked his lips. "Maybe I'll just take what is already running down your arm."

He held her hand and gently lapped up the blood dripping from her wrist.

In the next moment, they were both startled by the sudden appearance of Hector. He wore a button down pajama top tucked into a faded pair of jeans, and a scabbard hung from his belt. His blond hair stuck up on one side, where it had been slept on.

"Back away, vampire," Hector commanded.

Jeno dropped Gertie's hand and jumped to his feet.

"Wait, Hector," Gertie said, also standing. "It's not what you think."

He pointed a finger at Jeno, and, shaking with anger, said, "She's lost more than a pint."

"He didn't do it," Gertie insisted. "Hector, listen to me."

"Quit trying to protect him." Hector unsheathed his sword. "He knows the rules."

The moonlight glinted on the blade of the sword, pointing now at Jeno. It reminded her of Alexander's fangs just before he…

Gertie's heart beat out of control. Too much was happening too fast.

"Do it," Jeno said. "I dare you to slice off my head and feel the wrath of Dionysus."

Gertie positioned herself between Jeno and the sword. "No one is slicing anybody's head. Come on, Hector. This isn't fair."

She didn't mean to read his mind, but when he looked down at her with hurt in his eyes, she couldn't hold back.

So you've chosen, then.

"This isn't fair," she said again.

"When I look at you, I see a girl who's been hurt by more than one vampire," Hector said between clenched teeth. "A bite on your neck, wrist, and leg, color drained. *That's* what isn't fair. The tramps need to pay."

"She came to me like this," Jeno said. "She entered the caves."

"You did *what*?" Hector growled.

Gertie stopped herself from entering his mind. "I was frightened. I wanted his help."

"Why didn't you come to *me*?" Hector asked.

Gertie didn't know what to say.

A shriek from a distant hill made all three turn their heads. Bright flames licked the night sky, like long, forked tongues. Laughter and shouts rang out.

"Speak of the devil," Hector said.

"What is it?" Gertie asked.

Jeno stepped beside her, so that she was now flanked by both boys, as all three gazed at the bright flames on the other side of the acropolis.

"Dionysus," Jeno said. "That's the location of his old temple, before he was forced underground."

Gertie used her extraordinary vision to get a closer look. When the hill blocked her view, she hovered up into the air about twenty feet.

"Wait! What are you doing?" Hector cried.

"Are those the Maenads and satyrs with him?" she asked of the thirty or so women and hoofed men dancing around the fire.

Jeno flew up beside her. "Yes. And among them is my mother."

152

"Which one?"

"You see the one with the longest hair?"

"The dark hair?" She was dancing with a satyr.

"Yes. That's her," he said sadly. "Though she does not acknowledge me."

"I'm sorry," she whispered.

Hector cleared his throat.

Jeno and Gertie looked down to see him with his sword sheathed and his arms crossed and his foot tapping impatiently.

"May I please take you home, Gertie?' he asked. "You aren't safe."

She glanced at Jeno.

You should go with him, Jeno said telepathically.

"But I want to see Dionysus," she objected. "Who in their right mind wouldn't?"

Suddenly Jeno dropped from their height and fell toward the ground. Hector reached out and caught him in his arms.

Gertie flew down and landed on her knees beside where Hector was laying Jeno out on the ground.

"He's going into a coma," Hector said, positioning Jeno's arms at his side. "He needs blood."

"We have to help him." She put her wrist to Jeno's lips, but Jeno, who was barely conscious, refused to open his mouth. "Please. You need this."

"You've lost too much already." Hector pulled his sword from its scabbard and cut the palm of his left hand. Then he held his hand to Jeno's lips.

Jeno drank from Hector's offered hand, hesitantly at first, and then more urgently. He pressed Hector's hand against his mouth and sucked hungrily. Hector allowed it.

When Jeno released Hector's hand, he opened his eyes, wiped his mouth, and said, "Thank you. Why did you do that?"

Hector didn't reply, but Gertie could hear his thoughts, even though she tried not to listen, and she was certain Jeno could, too.

If you had harmed Gertie, I would have killed you; but you are clearly her friend.

Gertie's esteem for Hector went up several more notches. Jeno glanced her way, having heard her thought.

The voices from the distant hill were now overshadowed by music playing from pipes and flutes, and it sounded as though the source of it all was closer to them. By the time the three had climbed to their feet, a troop of dancers and players came around the hill in their direction.

"We need to get Gertie out of here," Jeno said.

"Agreed." Hector took Gertie by the hand.

But she didn't want to leave. She wanted to meet the satyrs and the god of the vine. She wanted to join their singing and dancing.

"I want to stay," she said.

154

"You'll end up like my mother," Jeno warned. "Come on."

Ten yards away, one of the Maenads pointed at them. She had the leg of a rabbit in the corner of her mouth—fur and all—and was sucking on it, as if it were a popsicle. Her hair was fire-engine red and piled on top of her head, with wild curls sticking out. Her face was pale, her eyes black, and two dark half-moons fanned from the bridge of her nose.

Tossing the rabbit leg to the ground, the Maenad screeched, "Ty yne afto?"

Gertie's vampire-infected mind understood that to mean, "What is this?"

Chapter Nineteen: Two Gods

As fast as a tidal wave, enormous vines grew out from beyond the hill and climbed along the rocks toward the three teens. Gertie drew in air and lifted herself from the ground, but the vines reached up and encircled her ankles before dragging her back down to the earth. She struggled against them, as they hauled her along the rocky ground toward the troop of Maenads and satyrs.

Jeno and Hector were dragged right alongside her. Hector pulled out his sword and swung at the vines until he freed himself. Then he charged after the other two, swinging and grunting, until he had freed them as well. Gertie and Jeno scrambled to their feet just as the troop caught up to them.

A satyr approached and offered them a goblet. Nubby horns stuck out through curly dark hair on the top of his head. His face was wrinkled but otherwise youthful, and his smile was disturbingly flirtatious. She glanced down at his hooves, wishing she could touch them to see if they were real.

"Don't drink," Hector warned.

Jeno gave her the same warning, telepathically, adding that it would turn her into a Meanad.

With her thoughts, she asked Jeno if the transformation would be permanent.

I don't know, he replied.

Gertie looked at the satyr. "What will happen to me if I drink the wine?"

"You will be set free," the satyr replied in the deep voice of an old man.

"From what?" she asked.

"From all that binds you," came his cryptic reply.

"Don't do it," Hector warned.

Please, Gertie, Jeno said, directly into her head.

"No, thank you," she finally said to the satyr, though her curiosity had nearly led her to take the cup.

She flinched when the satyr dropped the goblet at her feet and took out his pipe to join the other players, who skipped and jumped about. The women swung their arms and hips and kicked their legs. Dionysus remained hidden from Gertie's view, somewhere at the back of the crowd, where she sensed his presence. She tried to read his thoughts, but an impenetrable wall surrounded his mind. The Maenads seemed to have no thoughts, and the satyrs thought only of music and dancing.

Jeno's mind was full of his mother—memories of when he was a boy before her transformation. She saw him tugging at the hem of her skirt when he was six years old as she baked a batch of cookies. Gertie realized how selfish she'd been and sent a telepathic message to Jeno that they should leave.

She and Jeno each hooked an arm beneath Hector's and lifted off the ground. Before they had gotten very high, another vine caught hold of their feet, and the commanding voice in the distance shouted, "Wait!"

The music and dancing stopped, and all eyes turned up to the three teens, hovering above the ground and bound at the ankles by vines.

"What is this?" the commanding voice called out.

The troop below them parted—satyrs on one side and Maenads on another. Down the center, from the back of the crowd, strolled a magnificent ram, the size of a rhinoceros, with golden fur and horns.

Dionysus, Jeno told her.

"Since when are demigods and vampires *friends*?" the golden ram asked.

Hector and Jeno exchanged looks, as Hector shouted, "Since tonight, Lord Dionysus. A mutual friend brought us together."

"If only more would follow your example, the people of Athens might live in harmony," Dionysus said. "The prejudice against vampires has harmed the city more than the vampires themselves."

"You are right, my lord," Jeno said. "But why do you hold us prisoner?"

"I do not."

The vines disappeared.

"Seeing you together reminds me of an ambition of mine from days of old," the ram said.

Gertie asked Jeno what was going on, but he only shrugged.

"I have always wished to instigate an uprising of the children of the night."

"An uprising, my lord?" Jeno asked.

"So that vampires could be liberated from their impoverished crypts and given respectable positions in the city."

Gertie wondered what this would mean. She was all for equality, but a vampire uprising?

Hector gawked. "The gods of Mount Olympus…"

"Would finally be forced to feel my wrath," Dionysus said. "It was one thing to remove my temple and put Athena's in its place, but it is another to deny my requests again and again for better living conditions for my people. Seeing you three has reminded me of a more hopeful future for my followers."

"But what about the mortals?" Hector asked.

"They've had plenty of time to recognize the subjugation of my people and have done nothing. Perhaps it's time the tables were turned."

"There's got to be another way," Gertie said, not having meant to speak.

A great bird, as large as a small plane, swooped down from the Parthenon and hovered above the crowd, its wings flapping slowly and gracefully. It was an owl—gray and glimmering, brighter than the moon. Gertie's mouth dropped open as she looked up at the magnificent creature, suspecting its true identity.

Athena, Hector said in her mind.

Hector had spoken to her telepathically? The vampire virus must be in his blood. Did that mean he could hear her thoughts?

Yes, he said.

So who is worse than a thief now? she thought.

The owl opened its beak and said, "Dionysus, god of the vine! How dare you speak of an attack on my people so close to my temple? You are deluded if you think I wouldn't defend them."

The golden ram reared back on its hind legs and brayed.

Suddenly the music blared once more over the hills near the acropolis. The great owl hooted with condemnation before flying off in the dark sky. Jeno, Hector, and Gertie followed Athena's lead and left the party for the rock below the Parthenon. Athena continued to fly toward the moon and out of sight. Gertie watched her until her vampire eyes could no longer see her.

Once they had landed and were recovering on the rock, Gertie gazed down at the troop, its music still audible to her vampire-enhanced ears from this distance.

"What just happened?" she asked the boys, who were shaking almost as much as she.

"Have you heard talk of this uprising?" Hector asked Jeno.

"Every other century, my lord speaks of it, but nothing ever comes of it. I wouldn't worry."

"Maybe it was the wine talking?" Gertie suggested.

"That would be nice," Hector said. "But Athena seemed to take it seriously."

"That was incredible." Gertie kicked her feet with excitement from where they hung over the ledge. "Scary, but amazing. I saw two gods in one night."

"You have a way of attracting their attention, don't you?" Hector said.

Gertie laughed.

"The sun will be rising soon, and you will not be feeling well," Jeno said to Gertie. "You need to go home and stay in bed all day tomorrow." He turned to Hector. "Can you help her?"

Hector nodded. "I'll make sure she gets home all right."

"But you are a son of Apollo's direct descendant," Jeno said. "Don't you have some of his healing powers?"

"How did you know that?" Hector asked.

"You forget how long I've been around. I know things. Can you help her?"

"Do you mean, like magical healing powers?" Gertie asked.

"They're very mild," Hector said.

"You couldn't save your dog," Jeno said. "Because he was too far gone. Thanatos, the god of death, was already coming for him. But you *can* heal."

"What's he talking about?" Gertie asked Hector.

Hector opened his mind to her, and there she saw him holding his mangled dog, Paris, in the street after a car had run over him. Hector had tried to use his powers, but his dog had died. If his mother had been home from the hospital, she might have saved Paris, for her power was far greater than his. He resented his mother a little. She was always at the hospital. *Always*.

"I'm sorry," Gertie said.

"I haven't tried to use the powers since that day," Hector said. "I haven't had the occasion or the need."

"Try with her," Jeno coaxed. "Erase the bite marks, so Marta and her family won't worry. Heal the cuts and bruises from the vines."

Hector pressed his warm hand to her wrist and closed his eyes. A hot, tingling sensation crawled across her skin. When Hector removed his hand, the bite mark from her wrist was gone.

You are amazing, she thought.

Hector blushed and Jeno frowned.

"I didn't know I could do that," Hector said.

"Now her leg and throat," Jeno said.

Hector put his hand on Gertie's throat, causing her heart to go wild. The close proximity of his face to hers was

162

electrifying. She tried to hold back her thoughts of attraction and arousal as she glanced unwillingly at his mouth, which twitched into a grin. She turned her eyes from him and met Jeno's sad gaze.

I'm glad he's helping you, Jeno said telepathically.

My body responds to you both, she told Jeno, though she knew Hector could hear her thoughts as well. *It doesn't mean anything.*

Hector's grin became a thin line as he moved his hands to her ankles and continued his healing touch. Although her body continued to respond to Hector, she kept her eyes trained on Jeno. Nikita was in love with Hector, and Jeno needed her more than Hector did. Once she was healed of her bites, cuts, and bruises, she turned to Jeno and kissed him on the lips.

"Please come for me tomorrow night," she whispered.

"You will still be weak," Jeno said.

"Please."

Hector climbed to his feet, his mood drastically altered. "We should go."

"Goodnight," she said to Jeno.

"Goodnight," the vampire replied.

She and Hector pushed off and flew across the breezy sky. Gertie glanced back more than once at the lone vampire perched on the rock. She couldn't be sure, even with her powerful vision, but he appeared to be weeping.

Chapter Twenty: The Fall Festival

Nikita bolted into the room and dropped her backpack on her bed. "Feeling any better?"

Gertie opened her eyes. She'd slept on and off most of the day, with her e-reader within easy reach beneath her pillow for her waking moments. She hadn't eaten a thing, even though Mamá had brought her broth twice, once in the morning and once in the afternoon. Gertie's stomach had been churning all day.

On top of her physical pain was the psychological: her mind was haunted by the memory of Alexander forcing her on the sand and sinking his teeth into her neck. As mean as people could sometimes be, no one had ever treated her like that. It had made her feel broken inside.

"I have some exciting news." Nikita sat on her bed. "I think it will cheer you up."

"Oh?" Gertie didn't bother to sit up. Her head felt like a train was running through it.

"Dimos wants to take you to the fall dance!"

Gertie frowned. "Seriously?"

"Oh-em-gee, Gertie! He's a hottie. How can you not be excited?"

"Are vampires allowed to go?"

Nikita's mouth fell open, and she sat there, glaring at Gertie.

"What?"

"How can you even ask that?" Nikita admonished.

"You don't know Jeno." Gertie closed her eyes. She was so weak. "He's different."

Nikita said nothing.

"Ask Hector," Gertie added.

"You think I should?" Nikita's voice perked up.

Gertie opened her eyes and realized Nikita had misunderstood. She thought Gertie had meant for her to ask Hector to the dance.

"Do you want to?" Gertie asked.

"Well, I don't think he'll ask *me*. He treats me like a sister." Nikita stood up and crossed the room, where she gazed at her own reflection in the full length mirror on the back of the door. "I need to show him another side of me." She smiled wickedly.

Gertie grinned—and would have laughed if she had had the strength.

"Do you have to be a student at the school to attend the dance?" Gertie asked.

"You're *serious* about asking Jeno?"

Gertie nodded.

Just then, both girls turned their heads at the sound of sobs in the bathroom across the hall. Nikita glanced with alarm at Gertie and then left the room. Gertie used the little bit of strength she had to climb from her bed and follow.

"Mamá?" Nikita asked, opening the bathroom door.

Gertie watched from the hallway as Mamá put her arms around Nikita.

"What's wrong?" Nikita asked.

"Let us go to your room," Mamá said. Then she noticed Gertie. "Oh, Gertoula, are you feeling better?"

"What's the matter, Mamá?" Gertie asked. "Did something happen?"

"Come with me, girls."

They followed Mamá into their bedroom, where she closed the door. Each girl sat on her bed. Mamá sat beside Nikita.

"Something must have happened today to Phoebe at school," Mamá said. "Did she seem different on the car ride home?" she asked Nikita.

Nikita shrugged. "She was quiet, as usual."

Mamá wiped her tears. "She had been making such good progress, you know, with the sign language her friend was teaching her. I was learning it from her, and I can't tell you how wonderful it has been these past few weeks to feel as though we are speaking again."

"Then why are you crying?" Gertie asked.

"Phoebe refuses to use her hands today," Mamá said through tears. "I don't know why. She won't even look at me. I wish I knew what was going on inside that troubled head of hers."

An idea came to Gertie. If she had vampire powers, she could read Phoebe's mind. At that moment, she decided she would find a way to take Jeno to the dance, and she would ask him to bite her while everyone was still awake. Then she could help the Angelis family solve the mystery around Phoebe's silence.

A few days later, Gertie went to school, even though she still felt like she'd been hit by a car, and was surprised when, during first period, Hector leaned over and whispered, "Any chance you'd go with me to the fall dance?"

She really hadn't thought he'd ask, knowing her feelings about Nikita and her wish to maintain harmony in the Angelis household.

"You already know the answer to that," she whispered back.

"It's not fair," he objected.

No, it wasn't. Gertie agreed. But life was anything but fair.

"Nikita wants to ask you," she said. "You should go with her."

"I want to go with you."

"I'm taking Jeno," she said.

Hector's brows shot up. "You can't bring him here, to the school."

"Why not? You know he's different from the other vampires."

Hector glanced around, as if making sure no one had overheard. Then he returned to the assignment on his desk, so she returned to hers.

Gertie was surprised again later that day when Nikita told her that Hector had said yes to her invitation to go with her to the dance. They were alone in their room after school. Gertie had never seen Nikita more excited.

"You're so lucky you have a date," Gertie said.

"You shouldn't have said no to Dimos."

"Help me get Jeno to come." Gertie gave Nikita the best puppy eyes she could manage. "Please? And keep it a secret from Mamá and Babá."

"I don't know." Nikita sat on her bed, a little deflated.

Gertie sat beside her. "Just think how much fun it would be to go dress shopping together." Gertie actually hated dress shopping, but she was feeling desperate.

"Mamá and Babá can't afford that. I'll just wear something of Mamá's."

"No, please. Let me take you shopping. I have a credit card, remember? No one needs to know. We'll say you borrowed one of my dresses. They'll believe us. You've borrowed all my other clothes already."

"You have such an amazing wardrobe."

"You can have anything of mine you want. Plus, I'll buy you a dress for the dance."

The corners of Nikita's mouth twitched into a smile. "Seriously? You would do that for me?"

"Of course." Gertie's heart rate increased as she realized Nikita was about to break. "We'll help each other. Okay?"

Nikita nodded. "Okay."

That night, Gertie lay in bed, hoping once again that Jeno would come for her. How else could she ask him to the dance? She missed his beautiful, sad face and the way she felt when he kissed her. She knew he stayed away because he didn't think she was falling in love with him like he was with her, but she was determined to show him otherwise. He was the most amazing person she had ever met, and she was dying to be with him again.

She reached out to him with her mind, hoping he was listening to her thoughts. *Please, Jeno. Please believe me. I want to be with you.*

A week later, Gertie and Nikita convinced Hector to drive them to the mall. Jeno had not come for Gertie, so she wasn't even sure if he would agree to go with her to the dance, but Nikita had been so excited since Gertie had told her about shopping for dresses that Gertie had decided to think optimistically. Klaus went along, too, so he and Hector could hang out while the girls did their shopping.

Although Gertie had always dreaded shopping with her mother—mainly because their tastes were different and because her mother never seemed to consider Gertie's opinion—she enjoyed trying on dresses with Nikita. Maybe it was her friend's excitement that made it fun for Gertie. She'd gone to a few of the malls in New York with friends from school, but there was something different about Nikita. The other girls always seemed to have hidden agendas that Gertie could never figure out, and their loyalties changed from week to week. Nikita was one of the most genuine people Gertie had ever met. She realized she'd never had such a good friend before.

"Definitely!" Gertie said of the clingy, purple dress Nikita wore as she stepped out of the fitting room stall. "That's the one. Don't you think?"

"I really do!" Nikita said. "I've never worn anything so beautiful."

"You look amazing in it," Gertie said.

"Are you sure you can buy this for me?"

"I'm positive. But you have to help me find something now, too."

Gertie's grandmother had always told her that Gertie looked best in cool colors—like blue, pink, and purple—so when Nikita insisted that Gertie try on a deep red dress with a tight bodice and flowing, shimmery skirt, Gertie held it up to her skin, uncertain.

"Your blond hair and blue eyes pop against that red," Nikita said. "This is the one. I'm sure of it."

So Gertie put it on. She was absolutely surprised by her reflection. Who knew she looked good in red?

"Told you!" Nikita said as Gertie stepped from her stall. "You look breathtaking."

In her bare feet, she left the fitting room area to get a better look at herself in the larger mirror just outside. As she was checking herself out, Hector and Klaus came around the corner. Klaus whistled. Nikita dashed back into the fitting room, not wanting to be seen in the purple dress by Hector before the night of the dance, but it was too late for Gertie.

"Is that the one you're getting?" Klaus asked. "Please say yes."

"You like it?" Gertie asked.

Klaus blushed and said, "What's not to like. Don't you agree, Hector?"

Gertie found it difficult to meet Hector's eyes. The longing in them was too much.

He cleared his throat and said, "Yeah. It's nice."

That night, Jeno finally came for her. As soon as she met him on the sidewalk in front of the Angelis apartment, she threw her arms around his neck.

"Thank God you came," she said. "What took you so long?"

"I wanted to make sure you were well rested." He swept her hair from her eyes. "You shouldn't miss so much sleep while you're still recovering."

"Can we go somewhere to talk?" she asked.

"My island?" His smile faded as soon as he'd read her mind. "He did it to you *there*?" Jeno closed his eyes and clenched his teeth. "Well, at least you'll never have to worry about Alexander again."

Gertie shuddered. "Why do you say that?"

"I told you what I'd do to him."

"You..." Gertie's mouth fell open and she was speechless. Had Jeno really killed Alexander?

"It's the law," Jeno said. "I reported him to Hector."

"Hector killed him?" Gertie folded her arms across her body, hugging herself.

"We both did." Jeno shrugged. "I needed his help and he was happy to oblige."

"The two of you really killed him?" The finality of death was too hard to accept.

"Alexander had a reputation. I should have reported him before." Jeno put his hands on her shoulders and moved his face nearer to hers. "Then you would have been spared. I'm so sorry he did that to you."

Gertie lifted her mouth to his, and he accepted her kiss. She closed her eyes as he wrapped his arms around her and held her close, helping her to forget.

"Let's fly to the Parthenon," she whispered. "I have something I want to ask you."

The Angelis apartment was a flurry of excitement three weeks later on the night of the dance. Nikita and Klaus had performed at the festival with Hector and the rest of the choir earlier that day, and Gertie had sat with Mamá and Babá and Phoebe. For the first time, she had felt like a part of a real family.

The choir had sounded amazing. The band and orchestra had also performed, as had the dancers and the theater club. The other school organizations, including the photography club, had raised money at booths, which had lined the sidewalks in front of the high school and around the fountain. Gertie had sold nachos for one hour with Hector. He hadn't given her a hard time about not going with him to the dance and had actually been in a brilliant mood. They had laughed together, like when she had first arrived to Athens. It was a relief to her, though it also filled her with another feeling she didn't quite understand. Maybe she just wasn't the kind of person who could ever be one hundred percent happy with anything.

Mamá and Babá went on and on about how nice Nikita, Gertie, and Klaus looked in their fancy clothes as they were about to leave for the dance.

"We are so lucky that you brought such beautiful dresses with you," Mamá said as she fawned over the girls. "And Klaus looks so handsome in Babá's suit. You all look so beautiful, don't they, Babá?" She kissed each of their cheeks.

Babá took lots of pictures and tried to convince Phoebe to come and get in the photos, too, but Phoebe had withdrawn herself. The youngest Angelis rarely came out of Mamá and Babá's room anymore. Gertie was anxious to learn what was going on inside that little girl's head.

Klaus drove the three of them in Babá's car across the city to Hector's house. Nikita wasn't ready to let her parents know that she had asked Hector to be her date. They had decided not to even mention dates so that Gertie wouldn't have to explain hers, either.

Jeno was waiting for her at Hector's house. As the two boys stepped from Hector's front porch and walked across the yard to meet them, Gertie nearly lost her breath. They both wore nicely cut suits and ties and black dress shoes. Their crisp white shirts gleamed against the dark black blazers. Their skin also glowed. One boy was pale and blond and shining in the moonlight, and the other was dark with twinkling black eyes and thick, curly hair.

As the two girls stepped from the car, Klaus asked Gertie, "Are you sure about this?"

He hadn't been told about Jeno. The girls had been worried he would spill the beans.

"Yes," Gertie said.

Klaus backed from the driveway, waving goodbye, and then went to pick up his date, leaving the other four alone in the moonlight.

They were silent and awkward as they climbed into Hector's car—Nikita in the front and Gertie in the back with Jeno. Gertie focused on keeping her thoughts trained on Jeno even though she noticed Hector glance at her more than once in his rearview mirror.

"You look beautiful," Jeno whispered beside her.

"So do you," she said.

He smiled. "That isn't the first time you've told me that. It's nice to hear."

"You know I speak the truth."

He squeezed her hand. "Thank you so much for this night. I can't remember the last time I attended an event among mortals. Wait, yes I can. It was thirty years ago, I believe."

"That's so sad."

"Yes. And this is a happy occasion, so let's not talk anymore about sad things."

Nikita made small talk with Hector up front, as Jeno and Gertie continued to whisper their private conversation.

"I see your thoughts about dancing," he said.

"I suck at it. I hope you don't expect…"

"I do, actually. I love to dance and haven't in ages. You must dance with me, Gertie."

"I don't know."

"Leave it to me. I will lead you. You will see."

She hoped she wouldn't disappoint him.

"Never," he said.

When they followed Hector and Nikita into the high school gymnasium, Gertie was delighted by how the building had transformed. The dimmed lights, disco ball, colorful strings of lights along the walls and tables, and bronze steampunk props gave a mystical quality to the atmosphere. A big banner over the stage read: "Dance Through the Ages," and beneath it was a live band. Currently, they were playing a big band sound, jazzy and spastic.

"I like this music," Jeno said.

Unlike Gertie, who worried about others detecting Jeno for what he was, Jeno took her hand and led her with confidence smack dab in the middle of the dance floor where no one else, not even the chaperones, were dancing.

"Give in to me with your mind," he whispered. "I can lead you."

She gazed into his eyes and allowed him to control her as they moved flawlessly around the center of the room dancing what she soon recognized was the Charleston. She was no longer aware of the other students and faculty watching from the sidelines. Everyone fell away, and it was just the two of them laughing and dancing to the music from the band on stage.

When that song ended and a new one began, Jeno said, "Oh, this is from Fred Astair. Let's keep going."

Gertie couldn't believe how easily she moved as Jeno told her mind and body what to do. He swung her around and around, making her dizzy with laughter, but when that song was over and another began, he said once again, "We have to dance to this one."

"Seriously?"

"It's by Glenn Miller. Come on!" His smile was contagious.

Before she knew it, they had danced to Bing Crosby, Elvis Presley, the Beatles, the Beach Boys, the Bee Jees, Jefferson Starship, Madonna, Michael Jackson, and Mariah Carey. Other students eventually joined them on the dance floor, but Gertie had barely noticed them.

"I need some water," she said when Celine Dione's *My Heart Will Go On* rang from the stage.

They found Hector and Nikita standing beside Klaus and Joy by the refreshments. Jeno found a cold bottle of water and opened it for Gertie.

"Nice moves," Nikita said.

Both Hector and Klaus had stiffened and had exchanged glances. Gertie wished she could read their minds. "Thank you," she said. "Jeno deserves all the credit, though."

"Klaus, can you move like that?" Joy asked.

"I'm afraid not," he said.

"I could help you with that," Jeno said.

Gertie clapped a hand down onto Klaus's shoulder. "Why don't you give it a try?"

Klaus glanced at Jeno, who gave an encouraging nod.

"Okay. Come on," Klaus said to Joy as he led her away.

The other teens watched as Klaus expertly moved Joy across the dance floor. Then Gertie noticed Jeno moving his fingers in subtle motions in front of him.

Incredulous, she wondered if Jeno was really helping Klaus to dance.

Jeno gave her a smile and a nod. "He asked me to."

"Who asked you to do what?" Nikita asked.

Jeno did not reply, but kept his focus on Klaus.

Gertie leaned closer to Nikita and explained what Jeno was doing.

"So that's why you looked so smooth out there," Nikita said to Gertie. "Jeno was helping you, too."

Even Hector seemed delighted by Jeno's puppeteering. It was quite entertaining, Gertie thought with a smile.

Eventually, Nikita convinced Hector to dance one dance with her. It was a slow song, and as he took her in his arms and held her close, Gertie felt her stomach tighten. Jeno reacted immediately with a frown.

"Let's go for a walk," Gertie suggested while Hector and Nikita and Klaus and Joy were still on the dance floor. "Klaus can handle the dance on his own from here."

Jeno broke his tie to Klaus, who immediately looked a lot less smooth as he swayed with Joy to the slow music. Gertie stifled a snicker as she led Jeno out of the gym and into the cool night by the fountain at the front of the school. A few others passed by. Some kids were already being picked up by a line of cars that had formed in the parking lot.

"I need to ask you a favor," Gertie finally said.

"Ah," he said, somewhat sadly. "I should have known."

"What do you mean?" Gertie asked.

"I should have known this night could not be as perfect as it seemed. Everything in my life comes with a catch."

"There's no catch."

"You asked me to the dance so I would bite you again," he accused.

She looked up into his doubting eyes. "I wanted to ask you to the dance way before I thought of asking for the favor." She opened her mind to him, allowing him to see her concern over Phoebe.

"This isn't the way to solve her problem," he cautioned.

"You could do it for me, then. Find out what's wrong with her."

"For such probing, I need eye contact."

"So?"

"I haven't been invited into their apartment."

"Then bite me. Please? I could help them—the whole family. They've done so much for me."

She stretched her chin up and rested it on his chin. "Please, Jeno? Just once more. You know you want to, anyway. I can tell."

"Of course I want to," he said with a sigh. "I want nothing more than the taste of your blood, except to be desired by you as a man."

"You can have both." She caressed his lips with hers. "Please say yes. It would make us both happy." She closed her eyes and kissed his throat, feeling the breath rush from his lungs.

She wrapped her arms around his neck and pressed her body against his, overcome by the sensation of his large stature, his strong arms encircling her waist, and his breath, though cold, against her.

He kissed her hard, and she melted into his arms.

Then he whispered, "Not here."

He waved his hand at the passersby and then lifted her up into the night sky. He flew with her away from the school, away from the city, back to the rock beneath the Parthenon.

Chapter Twenty-One: Third Bite

The night was cold. Gertie shivered in Jeno's arms, but he could do nothing to warm her. She distracted herself with the beautiful lights of the city, which looked much like the stars above them. When they landed on the rock, Jeno took her into a tight embrace.

"My poor baby," he said. "You are so cold."

He moved his hands up and down her arms, trying to create heat.

"I've missed you so much," Gertie said. "Why don't you come see me more often?"

Jeno frowned. She wished she could read his mind.

That made him smile. "I'm trying to—how do you say— proceed with caution. You frighten me, koureetsi mou— especially in this red hot dress. It's my favorite color."

"How?" Frightened seemed like a strong word.

"It's not nearly strong enough. I can't get you out of my mind. I think about you every moment of every day. This is not good for you *or* for me. We need to take things slowly."

"Why?" She bit her lip. "I don't understand."

He gazed at her mouth, as though anticipating blood. He snapped his attention back to her eyes and said, "We must both make it past the lust."

"Lust?" Although she thought he was hot and she wanted badly to kiss him, she wasn't ready for sex.

He chuckled at her thoughts. "Your lust for my *power* and my lust for your *blood*."

"I don't lust for your power," she said.

"Isn't that why we are here tonight?"

"We are here tonight because I want to help the Angelis family."

"Let me tell you something, koureetsi mou," he said softly. "You remember the woman I told you about, the one whose deathbed I was leaving as I met you on the bus?"

Gertie nodded.

"How many times in the thirty years I knew her do you think I drank her blood?"

"I don't know. Hundreds of times?"

He shook his head. "Not once."

"Why not?"

"One taste of her blood, and I wouldn't be able to get enough. It's easy sometimes to confuse love and lust. I wanted to *love* her. And I did."

"You knew her thirty years, and you never drank her blood?"

"Not until the night she was dying, and then only because she asked me to."

"She wanted to become a vampire?"

Jeno sighed. "No. She knew how hard such an existence can be. She never wanted that."

"Then why?"

"Because she loved me, and because she wanted me to have her blood in my veins as she was leaving this world for the next."

"Oh." Gertie looked out over the city below. Now she wished she had never asked Jeno to bite her. No—she was glad she had. To experience his amazing powers was something she could not regret. And after one more bite, she would never ask for another. She just needed one more night of mind reading. She bit down hard on her lip and turned to Jeno.

He stared with longing at the blood beading there. "You did that on purpose."

"Kiss me." She reached her mouth to his.

He cupped her face in both hands and gently licked her lips. A moan escaped his throat as he pressed his mouth hard against hers. She felt him trembling as his touch turned feverish. He ran his hands from her cheeks to her neck, pressing his thumbs against her pulse. She had aroused him past the breaking point.

"Indeed," he whispered right before he sank his fangs into her throat and drank.

The bright stars in the sky turned into swirls and swirls of light, spinning like the images at the end of a kaleidoscope. Gertie felt so light and airy. Was she floating?

"Thee moy." Jeno wiped the excess blood from his mouth onto the back of his hand and then licked his hand clean.

Gertie had barely noticed. So many sounds and images and scents were hitting her all at once.

"Are you okay?"

She closed and opened her eyes as she was assaulted by his thoughts.

This was a mistake. She is overwhelmed.

"I'm okay."

The spinning lights finally settled into a fixed point, and she could now see that the stars were more than light. She could see they were distinct bodies, and outer space was full of many moving objects. She felt small and insignificant, but for only a moment, for her eyes then moved to the earth itself and to all the houses and cars and people below, and she felt like a powerful being among them.

I am *a powerful being.*

"Yes," Jeno said. "But don't let it go to your head."

His last word reminded her of her purpose. She needed to get inside Phoebe's head. It was time to discover what was preventing Phoebe from speaking, and what had lately made her withdraw more than usual.

"Are you sure you want to do this?" he asked her. "Some things are better left unknown."

"I'm sure. Can you help me?"

He stepped behind her and wrapped his arms around her waist. She leaned her back against him and tried to relax.

"Focus on the Angelis apartment," he coached.

"Yes, I'm looking at it now."

"Can you sense the little girl? She is walking around in the kitchen."

"Oh. Found her."

Gertie reached into Phoebe's mind, searching her memories. Phoebe's indecision about what she wanted to drink was getting in Gertie's way.

"How can I read beyond her current thoughts?"

"It's better to be close to her, so you can look into her eyes."

Gertie hadn't anticipated having to face Phoebe, but she'd gone this far. She couldn't give up now. "Will you go with me?"

"Of course."

They held hands as they flew. Gertie was no longer cold. In fact, now that the dizziness had worn off, she felt strong, energetic, and focused.

I am a powerful being, she thought again.

"This is true," Jeno said. "Even without the vampire virus in your blood."

Gertie didn't think so. It was a nice thing for Jeno to say, but she knew it wasn't true.

"You have to believe in yourself," he said.

She read the string of thoughts that followed.

This beautiful, intelligent girl has no self-confidence. Her parents have ripped her limbs from her body, too. Did they

185

know what they were doing to their daughter? Or were they like my mother—driven by forces beyond their control?

"You have such deep thoughts," she said, and was unable to stop her own: *for a vampire.* "I didn't mean that. You have deep thoughts for anyone, for any kind of being."

She covets my powers but abhors my race, just like everyone else.

"No. that isn't true! I don't abhor your race. I love vampires, remember?"

Fictional ones, his mind accused.

They arrived and landed on the sidewalk in front of the Angelis apartment.

"No. You do believe me, don't you?" she asked.

"You have good intentions," Jeno said. "But your attitudes betray you."

Gertie frowned.

"It's okay," he said. "I loathe myself and my race, too."

Gertie grabbed the lapels of his blazer in both fists and brought him close. "I could never loathe you, Jeno. I'm falling in love with you."

He made no comment, but his thought was, *We shall see.*

Gertie sighed. "Can you come with me?"

"The rules governing the ways of vampires are strict," Jeno said. "I have to be invited into a home before I can enter it."

"I'm inviting you."

"You are a guest. I don't know if that counts."

"Hmm."

"I'll be right here, koureetsi mou. You can do this."

"What exactly am I doing?"

"Sit with the girl, and look into her eyes. Look deeply, and you will find what you are looking for."

"I can't be seen by Mamá and Babá. They think I'm still at the dance."

"Take off your clothes."

Her eyes widened. "What?"

"Use invisibility, until you're alone with Phoebe."

"But then when I appear to her, I'll be naked." *That would certainly freak her out.*

"Use an illusion to cover yourself."

"How do I do that?"

There's not enough time to teach you. "I'll do it for you. Now take off your clothes and go, before the dance ends."

Reminding herself that he had x-ray vision anyway, and turning with embarrassment away from her own x-ray view of him, she pulled her energy inward—just like a turtle into its shell, until she could no longer see herself. Then she slipped out of the red dress and handed it to him.

He laughed at her. "Your underwear, too. Unless you want your bra and panties to appear to be floating around on their own."

She slipped out of them, her face red hot with mortification, and handed them over, too.

187

"Shoes," he said.

She bent over to undo the strap, but couldn't without seeing her own fingers.

"Let me help you," Jeno said.

He crouched at her feet and unbuckled her straps. Then he slid off each shoe. It was sensual and sad at the same time. She felt like Cinderella in reverse.

She shuddered. "Thank you."

"My pleasure," he said. "And stop already with the embarrassment. I can't see you when you're invisible. Besides, I can see through your clothes anyway."

"Like that helps." She laughed nervously.

Someone is coming. He balled up her clothes and hid them inside his blazer. He left her red pumps on the steps.

I'm terrified. She couldn't hide her thoughts. *What if I get caught?*

You don't have to do this.

Yes, I do.

She flew up to one of the opened windows and climbed inside, right by the television. It was on, and Mamá and Babá sat together on the sofa watching it. As quietly as she could, she crept from the room and down the hallway, looking for Phoebe.

Chapter Twenty-Two: Phoebe

The youngest member of the Angelis family lay on her cot in Mamá and Babá's bedroom watching a video on Babá's phone.

Before making herself visible, Gertie asked Jeno to remember to give her an illusion of clothes.

No worries, he said.

She stifled a laugh. Here she was, sneaking into her host family's apartment, naked, invisible, and using vampire powers to read the mind of its most fragile member, and Jeno was telling her no worries.

You don't have to do this, he repeated.

Gertie stepped back into the hallway, checked to make sure neither Mamá nor Babá were in sight, and then released her energy from its turtle shell. She was astonished to see herself in the same dress she had just given to Jeno.

You're good, she said to him.

I've had a little practice.

Phoebe noticed her as soon as Gertie re-entered the room.

"Hi, Phoebe," Gertie said, as casually as she could. "Mamá and Babá don't know I'm here. I wanted to ask you something."

Gertie had never spoken directly to her, so she was surprised when a look of panic crossed the girl's face. Phoebe dropped the phone on the cot and moved to the corner of the room, with her back against the wall.

"Don't be scared," Gertie said. "I just want to talk."

Phoebe did not seem comforted. She continued to glare back in horror at Gertie.

At least she's looking into my eyes.

Look deeply, Jeno said. *Make her look deeply into your eyes, too.*

"Look deeply into my eyes," Gertie commanded, gently.

Phoebe's eyes locked onto hers. The little girl flattened against the wall, her heart pounding out of control, and her mouth strained open, as though she were silently screaming.

Gertie was wracked by guilt for putting her little friend through such terror. "No need to be afraid, Phoebe."

Gertie looked beyond her friend's eyes, deep into her brain, and was shocked by the vision that began to unfold before her.

Gertie was lying in a bed in a room filled with smoke. Across from her, a toddler stood in a crib, gripping the rails.

Damien.

He had thin, dark curls on his round little head, and his dark eyes were blinking against the smoke. The pacifier he'd been sucking on fell out of his mouth and onto the hardwood floor.

Gertie found it difficult to breathe. She looked near the closed door to the source of the smoke. A fan was making a grinding sound and sparks and flames shot from its motor. One spark shot out and leapt onto the curtain just above Damien's crib. The entire window was soon in flames.

Gertie wanted to scream, but no sound came from her throat. She lay there, paralyzed with fear.

Damien fell down on his bottom in the crib. He choked out a cry, and then he disappeared behind a veil of smoke and flames. Gertie tried once more to scream.

The door to the room swung open. Babá met her eyes with a look of horror and shouted at her to get out, but Gertie couldn't move. Then he began a horrid dance with flaming blankets and pillows as he struggled to rescue Damien. The baby's body was limp in Babá's trembling arms as he headed for the door.

"Elate mazy mou!" Babá shouted, which Gertie now recognized as, "Come with me!"

Babá ran through the door, but Gertie was still paralyzed and now barely able to breathe. Seconds later, Mamá ran to the bed and swept Gertie into her arms. She rushed from the apartment and out onto the street, where Babá stood with Damien, who was badly burned and no longer moving. She hoped with all her heart that he was sleeping.

Mamá sat Gertie up on her feet and rushed to Damien. Her ear-splitting shriek made Gertie lose her balance and fall onto the curb.

Gertie looked for Nikita and Klaus and saw them screaming near the building for everyone to get out. Others ran down the steps and into the streets, coughing up smoke.

"Na me voithísei!" Mamá shouted into the dark night. Gertie understood it to mean, "Help me!"

Then Gertie had a shock. Mamá added, "Jeno, na me voithísei! Sas iketévo!"

Jeno?

Yes, koureetsi mou. Marta called to me, and I came. Let's go now. You know what happened.

Gertie wasn't ready to go. She continued to gaze into Phoebe's eyes and relive that awful night.

Jeno appeared beside Mamá.

"Save my baby! Please, Jeno!"

"I cannot *save* him," Jeno said gently. "I can only turn him."

"Do it!" Mamá cried.

"No!" Babá shouted, looking at the others with them in the street. In a lower voice, he asked, "Marta, are you crazy?"

"Is everyone out?" a neighbor cried in Greek.

"That's everyone," someone else confirmed.

Klaus and Nikita came and sat on the curb beside Gertie—one on each side of her. They huddled together. She could feel them trembling, could see them sobbing. Other people also sat on the curb, and others stood in the streets. No cars went by this late. It was the middle of the night.

Gertie thought she heard sirens in the distance. Someone must have called for help.

"Is Damien..." Nikita started to ask, and then didn't.

Mamá held Damien protectively and stepped away from Babá. "Would you rather let him die? I can't. I'm not ready to let my baby go!"

"This isn't the way," Babá said gently.

"Please, Nico! I beg of you! Just for a little while! Just long enough for me to hold him and speak to him and sing to him. Please, oh, God, please!"

Gertie was sobbing now, too. She couldn't stand to see Mamá in such pain. She wanted to say, "Please, Babá!" but once again, she could not speak.

"It's against the laws," Jeno said to Mamá.

"If you ever loved me," Mamá said fiercely, "do this for me!"

Babá rushed to the curb where Gertie sat between Klaus and Nikita. "Not in front of the children."

"There's no more time," Jeno said. "Damien will soon be cold."

"Do it now!" Mamá begged. "Stupefy these others, as I've seen you do before. Please, Jeno!" She handed the limp form of Damien over to Jeno, whose eyes flickered with hunger.

Jeno took the baby into his arms. Gertie saw his fangs protract just as he bent over Damien. The sight made her shudder. Babá tried to shield them from what was happening, but all three children watched with unbelieving and horrified faces as the vampire drained little Damien of blood.

Within a matter of seconds, Damien, whose cheek and neck were burned on one side, opened his eyes and sat up in Jeno's arms. "Mamá?" He looked around the crowd for his mother.

His tiny voice brought joy to Gertie. She smiled and jumped to her feet. Tears streamed from her eyes as she ran toward the little boy, still in Jeno's arms.

"Damien!" she cried.

Damien turned his sweet little face toward her and smiled. But then his mouth snapped open, revealing sharp fangs. Before Gertie could react, Damien flew at her and knocked her down onto the street. Sharp pains stabbed at her, all over her body. Damien was mauling her! He bit her face, her neck, her chest, and her wrist. He finally settled on her wrist, sucking up her blood. Gertie was surrounded by a frenzy of screams and people tugging her and Damien every which way. Finally Jeno took Damien with brute force.

The sound of sirens, the smell of smoke, and the blurry sight of colorful lights and bright red flames overwhelmed Gertie. She blinked against the spinning air. She felt dizzy and terrified.

Are you okay, koureetsi mou?

Who is talking?

It's me, Jeno. Come away, now.

But what happened to Damien?

Gertie looked deeply into Phoebe's eyes, deep into her brain. The scene changed.

She stood between Klaus and Nikita in the basement of the Angelis's current apartment building. On the floor in front of them were two coffins. The larger one was closed and heavily chained. The smaller one was opened.

Gertie took a step and leaned over the lip of the coffin. It was Damien.

"Say goodbye, koureetsti mou," Mamá said through tears.

"Is he dead?" Nikita asked.

Mamá exchanged a troubled look with Babá, who said, "No. Just sleeping."

Suddenly, Gertie was the one lying in the coffin. Her eyes were closed, but she could sense everyone in the room. She could also sense it when the coffin lid was closed on her. She heard the chains being secured and the click of the lock as it was fastened.

Then she sensed a small hand touch the coffin lid, and that spark of humanity made her open her eyes and beat on the lid in a state of panic and terror. Screams echoed throughout the room.

"Don't touch it!" Mamá cried.

Once the hand left the wood, the spark left her body. She realized as she lay there, no longer able to move, that the hand had been Phoebe's. She could sense everything Phoebe did and said, and she could tell that Phoebe could sense Gertie, too.

But that one comfort was not enough to quell the terrifying fact that she was trapped in a coffin with no hope of escape. As she sensed the Angelis family leaving her there all alone—not alone, there was another presence with her—the gripping realization that they would never let her out made her want to scream.

She strained, but she could not open her mouth. She could not move a muscle. She could only lie there, buried in the coffin, alive.

A loud shriek brought Gertie from the vision. Phoebe stood across the room, still flattened against the wall in the corner, but she had broken eye contact and was screaming frantically as tears poured down her face.

As soon as Gertie realized that Mamá and Babá were coming, she pulled all her energy inward, attempting to make herself invisible. But the trauma of the vision had drained her of strength, and she fumbled with it. She saw herself shimmering, like a hologram in a science fiction flick.

Mamá crossed the room to Phoebe and took her daughter in her arms. "What is this?"

Babá glared at Gertie. "What have you done?"

"Tramp stamp!" Mamá cried, pointing at Gertie's neck and clinging to Phoebe. "She's possessed!"

"How could you?" Babá demanded. "We welcomed you into our home, made you a part of our family. How could you betray us this way?"

"I wanted to help!" Gertie insisted. "Mamá, Babá, please listen. You don't understand."

"Don't you know that Phoebe has already been through enough?" Mamá accused. "Confronting her in this way, this is not help!"

Phoebe buried her face in her mother's embrace and sobbed.

"Get out of my home!" Babá shouted to Gertie. "And don't come back until you're yourself again. I can't stand to see you this way!"

"But..."

"Go!" Mamá cried. "Just go! And when you come back, you can pack your things. We're sending you back to America!"

Gertie's stomach twisted into a knot. "What? No, please! I was only trying to help!"

Come away, koureetsi mou, Jeno called to her. *Let them recover from their shock.*

Chapter Twenty-Three: The Story of the Other Coffin

Gertie ran from the room and flew out of the window, to where Jeno was waiting for her. He took her in his arms and helped her back to the rock beneath the Parthenon.

"Why didn't you tell me?" she shouted at Jeno.

"I tried to," he said. "But you seemed determined to do this. And I didn't know the full story. I wasn't even sure if that's why the girl won't speak."

She couldn't believe how things had turned out. She'd only been trying to help, and now she'd ruined everything. The only family that had ever loved her now hated her. They were shipping her back to her parents, who'd never wanted her in the first place.

"The Angelis family doesn't hate you," Jeno said, as he helped her into her clothes and shoes.

"You didn't see their faces."

"They're in shock."

She flapped her hands in the air like a bird. "They're sending me back. What am I going to do?"

"Give them time to recover." He took her hands and kissed them.

"I'll run away before they send me back. I don't want to leave you." She didn't want to leave Nikita or Klaus or Hector, either.

"Take a deep breath and calm down."

She paced around the rock. "I'm too worked up. I can't shake the feeling of being in that coffin. Poor Damien. He's trapped in there!"

"He's in a coma."

"No." Gertie shook her head. "I saw inside his head."

"That's impossible."

"Phoebe has some kind of psychic connection to him. She can hear his thoughts and sense his feelings, and he can sense hers."

"What?"

"I'm telling you, Jeno. It was like I was inside Damien's body, even though I was really inside Phoebe's head. That's why she can't speak. She's continually traumatized by Damien's entrapment. He may not be able to move or to speak, but he's aware. He's not in a coma."

"Thee moy," Jeno said, sinking onto the rock. He sat on the edge, allowing his legs to hang over the side. "I can't believe it."

"What's even worse is the other vampire in the coffin beside him. Damien is terrified of him."

"But he shouldn't be. Damien has no reason to fear my father."

Gertie's mouth dropped open. "Your father?"

Jeno patted the rock beside him. "Come sit with me."

Although Gertie still felt spastic, she did as he had asked. She swung her legs over the edge, back and forth, as though she were kicking her demons away.

"Why is your father in the Angelis's apartment basement?"

Jeno opened his mind to her and started to show her his memories.

"No more flashbacks. Please," she said. "I've had enough for one night."

"Remember how I told you my mother killed my sister and father and me?"

Gertie nodded.

"And then Dionysus was ordered by Zeus to repair our bodies?"

"Uh-huh."

"And I told you my father refused to drink human blood, which was how he went into a coma?"

"Yes?"

"Though now, if what you're saying is true of *all* vampires, he's not really been in a coma." Jeno winced. "My poor father. And poor little Damien."

"Go on, Jeno."

"Well, just like every vampire, my father went crazy for human blood when he was first made. He could not control his blood lust—just like Damien couldn't the night he attacked his sister."

"I'm so sorry." Gertie couldn't imagine the feeling of being so out of control, as to hurt the ones you love without meaning to.

"My father and sister and I, along with the families of the original Maenads, are the first generation of vampires, but when we were formed, we created a second generation. Literally hundreds of new vampires were created during our blood lust."

"So what does that mean?"

"Well, in every century, there is usually a group of humans that wants to destroy my kind, and they eventually learn that by killing *my* generation—me and my father and sister and so on—they will destroy all vampires."

"What? Is that really true?"

"Yes. In fact, the newest vampires can even be restored to their original form, as long as they were heathy when they were turned."

"You mean they can be human again?"

"That's right." *Though, that wouldn't have worked for Damien.*

Because he was already dying.

Exactly. And it wouldn't work for vampires who have lived beyond their human lifespan. Their bodies degenerate immediately.

Gertie cocked her head to the side. "You know this from experience?"

"I've seen it happen many times. Whenever a vampire breaks the law and is destroyed by a demigod, all that vampire's most recent victims are restored. The older ones die away. And any vampires *they* created also either die or are restored."

"So what does this have to do with your father being in the Angelis's apartment basement?"

Jeno squeezed Gertie's hand. "When I turned Damien, I broke the law."

"That's right. So it wasn't reported?"

"No, it was. Two of the firemen who put out the fire that night were demigods, and I couldn't stupefy them. They saw what I'd done, and they couldn't be made to forget."

Gertie covered her mouth. "Oh, no. So what did you do?"

"Marta came to my defense and admitted her part in it all. The firemen were sympathetic, and one of them even agreed that I should be spared, but they wanted Damien destroyed."

"Why?"

"They had seen his attack on his sister. They knew that vampire babies are the most deadly. They have incredible strength and no self-control. Usually their victims don't even see them coming."

"It would have been better for Damien if they *had* destroyed him. He's been trapped and terrified all these years."

"You mustn't tell Marta," Jeno said. "You will break her heart."

"Okay."

"Promise me," he said urgently.

"I promise." Then she asked, "But what about Damien?"

Jeno put an arm around her waist and pulled her closer to his side. "Thee moy, yes. We must think of something. And for my father, too."

"So, anyway, how were you and Damien spared?"

"The two demigods, Marta, and I, with Damien in my custody since he was a danger to everyone else, appeared before the court on Mount Olympus."

"You what? Are you kidding me?"

"I speak the truth. I swear."

"You saw the gods? You saw Zeus and Athena and Aphrodite?"

"Not in their true form," he replied. "They took the shape of their animals. Zeus was a mighty eagle."

"And he spoke to you?"

"Oh, yes. He yelled at me."

"But you were only trying to help."

"He said I should have known better. And I should have."

"What else did he say?"

"He said that Damien would have to be either destroyed or deprived of blood until he went into a vampire coma, and then he must be bound into a tomb without the possibility of escape."

"So that's why he's there. What about your father?"

"Lord Zeus also said that the vampires would have to give up my father's body to be placed in the custody of humans. This would ensure that the humans would have leverage against any attempt by the vampires to break the laws. One stake through my father's heart would kill all but the first generation of vampires."

"What's to stop anybody from doing that now? Aren't you worried someone will sneak into the basement and destroy your father?"

"That's where Hector comes in."

"Hector?"

"The gods assigned him to be a protector and enforcer of their ruling. He makes sure Damien remains entombed, and he also protects my father."

Nikita had said he was their protector. She had meant her family, not the vampires. "And does he also protect the Angelis family?"

"Yes. And the other mortals living in that apartment."

"From what?"

"From vampires wanting to return my father to the caves below us."

"And they would want to do that to ensure their own safety, right?"

"Right." *And to ensure the success of an uprising.*

"Uprising?"

"You heard my lord, Dionysus, the other night. He speaks of one every so often."

"Do you think he was serious this time?"

"I don't know. I've heard talk among the caves. And if he was, the first thing the vampires would do is…"

"Rescue your father's body."

"And to do that, they would have to…"

"Get past Hector."

"They would probably kill him," Jeno said.

Gertie laid her head on Jeno's shoulder. "You can't let that happen."

"I'll do what I can, but I'm only one vampire."

"You'd be sure to warn Hector and the Angelis family, though, right? If you ever heard news of such a thing?"

"Of course." He stroked her hair. "But let's not worry about that right now."

"No, you're right. We have enough already, like what I will do about Mamá and Babá. They can't make me leave, Jeno." Tears spilled from her eyes.

Chapter Twenty-Four: Banished

Gertie returned to the Angelis apartment just before dawn and quietly slipped into bed. She slept for two hours before she was awakened by Mamá's voice telling the girls that one of them should go to the shower.

It was like the events of last night hadn't happened.

But as soon as she saw the looks on Babá and Mamá's faces at the breakfast table, she knew what had happened had been more than a bad dream. Mamá handed her a scarf and told her to quickly cover her stamp.

Nikita came to the table just as Gertie had put on the scarf. "Where's Phoebe?"

"She's not well," Babá said. "She's staying home today."

Nikita looked at Gertie's scarf with suspicion, but said nothing.

During the car ride to school, the other three teens wanted to know where Gertie and Jeno had gone during the dance.

"We looked all over for you," Nikita said. "I was worried."

"We all were," Hector added.

Gertie couldn't decide whether to tell them the truth, or to pretend as though nothing had happened. She chose the truth.

"I thought I was helping," she said, after she had finished relaying what had happened. "And I did learn something important. I know why Phoebe can't speak."

"What?" Klaus asked. "What do you mean?"

"What are you talking about?" Nikita asked beside her in the back seat.

"Phoebe has a psychic connection to Damien," Gertie said. "She can sense him. And he's not in a coma. He's fully aware of his surroundings, of his entrapment. He's miserable and terrified, and Phoebe can constantly sense that. His silent screams make her silent."

At first the car was deathly quiet. Gertie supposed they were all in shock. Moments later, Nikita burst into tears. Klaus did, too.

"Poor Damien," Hector said, as he turned into the school. "Are you sure?"

"I'm absolutely positive," Gertie said. "I could feel it through Phoebe's mind."

"Poor Phoebe! Poor Damien!" Nikita wailed—her face twisted in utter grief. "Oh, Hector. Please take me home. I can't go to school today. I just can't!"

"Me, too," Klaus said through his tears. "God, this is unbearable. My baby brother and sister have been in constant agony for three years. Pull over. I'm going to be sick."

Hector did as he was asked. First he pulled over, and then he took the Angelis kids back home. Gertie and Hector followed them up to the apartment. None of them would go to school today.

When they walked inside, Mamá and Babá turned from where they sat together on the sofa.

"What are you doing home?" Babá shouted with surprise.

"Why aren't you in school?" Mamá climbed to her feet.

Nikita ran into her mother's arms. Klaus fell onto the nearby chair.

"Gertie told us about last night," Hector explained.

Mamá narrowed her eyes at Gertie. "So it wasn't enough to upset Babá and Phoebe and me? You had to upset them as well?"

"You don't understand," Nikita said. "She found out why Phoebe can't talk."

Mamá's eyes widened with surprise. "What?"

Babá jumped to his feet. "Is this true?"

Gertie wished she could disappear. She had promised Jeno not to let Mrs. Angelis know the truth about Damien's suffering.

Gertie shook her head. "No. I mean, I'm not sure."

Now Klaus was on his feet. "You said you were absolutely positive."

"So which is it?" Nikita asked. "Do you know or not?"

"What did she say?" Mamá asked Nikita.

"Don't tell her," Gertie said. "It will only hurt her."

"She needs to know," Klaus said. "Both of my parents need to know, so they can do something about it."

"Tell me," Babá demanded.

"I'm really not as sure as I thought," Gertie back tracked. "It might have been a hallucination. The vampire virus might have been messing with my mind."

"Now *that* I believe," Babá said. "Which is exactly why it's time to get you away from here."

Now it was Gertie's turn to burst into tears. "Please, don't make me go. I'm sorry. I won't do it again."

"That's what you said last time," Mamá pointed out. "This is for your own good. We warned you about addiction."

"I'm not addicted!" Gertie shouted. "I was trying to help you. All of you. I wanted to find out what was wrong with Phoebe."

"But we already know what is wrong," Babá said. "We know what she went through the night of the fire. We didn't need you to dredge up those memories for her again."

"Gertie said Phoebe has a psychic connection to Damien," Klaus said. "She can sense him."

"That's impossible!" Mamá shouted. "And I've heard enough. There will be no more discussion about this."

"Nikita, go and help Gertie pack her bags," Babá said. "We've already called the Morgans. Her tickets for her way home have been purchased."

"You leave tonight," Mamá added. "This is better for you and for us. I hope you understand."

Gertie did not understand. She and Nikita went to their room, where they hugged and cried in each other's arms.

"Why didn't you tell them the truth?" Nikita asked. "Or *was* that the truth?"

"I promised Jeno I wouldn't tell your mother. He said it would break her heart."

"She needs to know. We have to help Phoebe and Damien."

"How?"

"I don't know."

They sat on their beds, facing each other. "I don't want to go back, Nikita."

"What choice do you have?"

"I could run away, here in Athens. Maybe Jeno could help me."

"He has no way of helping. He might be able to protect you from other vampires, but he can't get you food or shelter."

"What about Hector?" Gertie asked, hesitantly.

Nikita didn't reply at first. She got up, paced the floor, and wringed her hands.

Finally, Nikita said, "Maybe Hector *can* help. His mom is rarely home."

"Ask him to come in here for a minute," Gertie said.

"What excuse will I give?"

"I can't reach something up in the closet?"

Nikita frowned, but she left and returned a moment later with Hector. Klaus was on his heels.

"Close the door," Gertie whispered.

Hector and Klaus glanced first at Gertie and then at Nikita, waiting for an explanation.

"She doesn't want to go home," Nikita said.

"I'm not going back," Gertie said. "I don't have a life in New York to go home to. My parents couldn't care less about me. I need to prove to Mamá and Babá that I belong here." Tears poured down her face. She had never loved her own parents as much as she loved Mr. and Mrs. Angelis.

"I don't think we can change their minds," Klaus said. "They are angry and hurt. And they're worried about you getting more and more addicted."

"I'm not addicted!" Gertie hissed. Then she covered her mouth, hoping her voice hadn't carried into the other room.

The four teens waited and listened for a backlash from the adults, and when none came, they turned back to their conversation.

"Can you hide me at your place?" Gertie asked Hector. "Just long enough for me to convince Mamá and Babá to let me stay?"

Hector's face turned bright red. "I'm not sure if my mom will allow it."

"We don't have to tell her," Gertie said.

"I don't like all this lying," Nikita groaned.

"Me either," Klaus added. "Why don't you go home for a few weeks, give my parents time to cool off? Then maybe we can convince them to let you come back next semester, after Christmas. I think they would let you come back, because they don't want us to get kicked out of the American school."

"And because they love you," Nikita added. "They're just hurt."

"That's right," Hector said. "Just go for a little while, and then come back."

Tears flooded Gertie's eyes and spilled down her cheeks. They didn't understand. They had no idea how she felt. They didn't get that *they* had become her family, and asking her to leave was breaking her heart.

Hector's expression softened, and he moved closer to her. "I suppose a day or two would be all right."

Gertie threw her arms around his neck and allowed all her fear and anxiety to pour out through her sobs. Hector held her for many minutes as she cried onto his shirt.

"I'll offer to take you to the bus station," Hector said gently. "We have a guest room, where you can stay."

Gertie turned to Nikita and threw her arms around her neck, just as she had Hector's. "Thank you for helping me. You're like a sister to me. I couldn't stand to leave you."

Nikita hugged her back, tears spilling from her eyes now, too. "We just have to be careful. We can't hurt Mamá and Babá. They're too fragile."

"I know." Gertie pulled away. "I promise to be careful."

Gertie went up to Klaus and hugged him. "Please don't tell on me. Please?"

"Okay, but just for a few days," he said, hugging her awkwardly. "I don't like to lie."

"I know, Klaus." She pulled away to meet his gaze. "And I appreciate that. I don't like to, either. I just need a couple of days to sort things out."

Nikita, Klaus, and Hector helped Gertie pack and get her bags ready near the door. After lunch, Hector went out to his car and got his ukulele, and they passed the rest of the day singing songs together in Nikita's room. Gertie couldn't be more grateful.

Hours later, before supper, Mamá knocked on the door and asked for a word alone with Gertie.

The other three teens left the room, and Mamá sat on Nikita's bed, across from Gertie.

Gertie couldn't even look at her. She clenched her teeth, trying to fight off the tears, but they flowed down her cheeks anyway.

"I'm sorry it has come to this," Mamá said. "Maybe our city is too hard for outsiders to navigate. It's too ancient. We have too many secrets."

Gertie wanted to say that she wasn't an outsider. In the past few months, this had become her city, too—her only true home. "Mamá, I'm sorry."

"I know that, Gertoula. But this is for the best. You need to get away from this unhealthy climate. Maybe one day you can come back and visit, no?"

How could Mamá let her go? Gertie felt in that moment that maybe she had come to love Mamá and Babá more than they had come to love her. The tears poured from her eyes like a waterfall.

"Please don't make me leave," Gertie begged.

Mamá sat beside Gertie and put her warm, comforting arms around her. Gertie buried her face in Mamá's shoulder and breathed in her smell, wishing she could stay in those arms forever. Did Nikita and Klaus realize how lucky they were to have such a loving mother? Gertie wished so badly that Marta Angelis had been her mother, too. She wished she could open her eyes and discover that life had been a bad dream and she had really belonged to this lovely family all along.

A roach darted across the floor, and Gertie didn't even flinch. She would take this roach-infested apartment over her luxurious mansion in New York any day.

"I'm afraid I've worried your mother," Mamá said. "She said you haven't kept in touch with her at all since you left, and she thinks it's best that you come home."

Gertie bit her lip. That was just like her mother—to blame their lack of communication on Gertie. Well, communication was a two-way street. When had her mother last texted her? It had been Gertie's first night in Greece, when she was on the bus from Patras. Three months ago.

"I'll miss you so much," Gertie muttered through wracking sobs. "I don't care about my mother and father. I care about you and Babá."

"Oh, please don't say such a thing, kouretsi mou!" Mamá hugged her more tightly. "That would break your mother's heart."

Gertie almost laughed, but she was crying too hard. She wanted to say, "Yeah. Right." But she held her tongue. Instead, she said, "I promise to stay away from Jeno. I'll have nothing to do with the vampires."

"I know you won't, because I'm removing you from the temptation." Mamá pulled away to look into Gertie's crying eyes. "This really is as much for your own good as it is Phoebe's."

"How is making me leave good for Phoebe?" Gertie asked.

"You must understand that I cannot risk her being reminded of her trauma. That's what happens every time she sees your tramp stamp."

215

Gertie covered her throat and started to speak, but Mamá continued, "She was making such good progress. And now we are back to square one."

Gertie threw her arms around Mamá's waist and cried harder than she'd ever cried in her life. "I'm so sorry!"

Mamá held her quietly for many minutes, and then she said, "We will keep in touch, no? And one day you will come back for a visit."

When Mamá stood up to leave the room, Gertie noticed that she had begun to cry, too. "We will miss you, Gertoula." Mamá fled the room.

Chapter Twenty-Five: Hector's Place

After dinner, Gertie hugged each member of the Angelis family—except Phoebe, who had refused to come out of Mamá and Babá's room since their shared vision—and then left with Hector and all of her luggage. She was less miserable, knowing that she wasn't really leaving and was convinced that she would eventually persuade Mamá and Babá to let her stay.

She had already hatched a plan to text her parents and tell them her plane had been delayed. She doubted they would check the flight status and discover her lie for at least two days, maybe three.

The ride to Hector's house was awkwardly quiet, until Hector popped in a CD and started singing along. Gertie was grateful for his good disposition and his beautiful, calming voice.

"Is this a Greek band?" she asked in between songs.

"This is *my* music," he said.

"What? Really? That's you singing on the CD?"

He nodded. "Ever hear of SoundCloud?"

"No. What is it? Like Youtube?"

"More like Facebook for music lovers," he explained. "I have a little following."

"I bet you do. How many followers?"

"A few thousand."

"What? Why didn't you tell me before?"

He shrugged.

"Do you ever spend time on Goodreads?" She cocked her head to the side. "It's kind of like Facebook for booklovers."

"Yeah. Are you on there? I post status updates at least once a week."

"Me, too!"

"I'll send you a friend request."

She took out her phone. "I'm sending you one now."

After they pulled into the driveway, Hector helped her haul her luggage up to the guest room, which was spacious and nicely decorated, much like her rooms back in New York City. At the foot of the queen-size bed were a loveseat and coffee table. Across from them was a television, and in the corner were a desk, a laptop, and a small bookcase full of books, games, and puzzles.

It seemed so big compared to the room she'd been sharing with Nikita, and yet she'd give anything to be back in that little room—roaches and all.

"Do you have a lot of guests stay here?" she asked.

"We used to when I was younger, but not anymore."

She glanced over the titles of the books. Most were nonfiction—not really her thing.

"Can I get you something to eat or drink? You want a snack?" he asked.

She was still full from supper. "No thanks." She turned from the bookcase and gave him a smile. "Thanks again for doing this for me."

He blushed. "You're welcome."

"I hope I won't get you in trouble."

"It's nothing I can't handle."

"Wanna watch some television with me before we go to bed?"

"Excuse me?" His blush deepened.

She felt her own face turn red. "I didn't mean we'd go to bed *together*. I meant…"

He laughed. "Oh. Okay. In that case, yes. Let's watch some television."

Gertie felt the awkward tension between them as they sat beside one another on the loveseat. Hector flipped through channels, but didn't have much luck finding anything they both cared to watch, so he put it on a music channel and told her about the band whose song was playing.

"Their songs are really soulful," he said. "This one's about breaking out of your fish bowl. It's my favorite."

The song was in Greek, so she couldn't understand it, but she liked the sound. And she enjoyed watching Hector try to translate it for her. They both laughed at how strange the translation was. She begged him to let her listen to more of his original compositions. He pulled out his ukulele and played one for her.

"Ooh. A live concert!" She clapped her hands. "I'll take it."

The melody was a slow ballad. His magnificent voice, deep and low, sang:

She has a way, she lifts me off the ground.

My head is spinning round and round.

My heart gets beating way too fast

As she walks past...

And she walks past.

From afar, I try to get the nerve

To go to her and say these words.

But my heart gets beating way too fast

As she walks past...

And she walks past.

She swallowed hard. "That's beautiful."

"You think so? I just now made it up."

"Wow." She wondered if the song was about *her*.

He put down his ukulele. "I have to tell you something."

She stiffened, stealing herself for whatever he was about to say.

"I told Nikita that I like you," Hector said.

"You what?" Gertie jumped from the loveseat and paced the room, thinking back to how Nikita had acted. Gertie hadn't noticed anything unusual in Nikita's behavior. "What did she say?"

"She seemed okay with it," he said. "She seemed disappointed, but she understood."

"Well, of course she's not going to say you broke her heart. She's too proud."

"I don't think I broke her heart. It was just a crush." He climbed to his feet and faced her, his hands shoved in the front pockets of his jeans. "I've never given her any reason to believe there was something more between us."

Gertie sucked in her lips. Hector was amazing. What was there not to like back? Of course she liked him—had liked him from the beginning—but she couldn't go there. She had to think of Jeno. The vampire needed her more than Hector did.

She had made promises to Mamá, but she couldn't just turn her back on Jeno. She had feelings for him. And yet, Hector was no longer off limits. Shouldn't she at least consider...Gertie sighed. She didn't know what to do.

"I know you're into Jeno." Hector's mouth twitched into a nervous smile. "I get that. I just want you to know that I'm here for you if you ever change your mind."

If Gertie had known that Hector had said something to Nikita, she never would have suggested he hide her out in his house. This was now so totally awkward. She paced around the room again.

"I'm sorry," he said. "I shouldn't have said anything."

She stared at the floor, because whenever she looked at him, her memory of that night in the sea flooded her mind. The taste of his lips, the feel of his skin… "No, it's okay."

"I guess I just thought that maybe," he took a deep breath. "I overheard you promise Mrs. Angelis that you would never have anything to do with Jeno or the vampires again."

Gertie met his gaze. "You were listening?"

"The walls are so thin. I didn't mean to. Everyone heard."

"Oh."

"Listen, I didn't mean to go down this road. Really. I'm going to leave you alone now before I make an even bigger fool of myself. Good night."

He walked out before she could think of anything to say.

Alone in the queen-size bed, she laid there talking to Jeno in her mind, hoping he was listening. She wanted him to know how much she still cared about him and how much she missed him. Although she knew he wouldn't, she asked him to come to her. Was he just going to sit idly by as Hector tried to woo her away from him? Or was Jeno going to fight for her?

The alarm on her phone woke her the next morning. The on-suite bathroom had everything she needed to get ready. Once she was dressed, she followed the hallway to Hector's room. They hadn't discussed how he was going to sneak her out of the house to school.

When she reached his room, she softly rapped on the door. He didn't answer, so she tapped a little harder. Still nothing.

She turned the knob and entered. "Hector?"

The morning sun bathed the room with light, washing over the unmade four-poster bed and matching side-table, where an opened book lay face down beneath a lamp. Some papers on the desk beneath one of the windows caught her eye. They were charcoal drawings. She stepped closer and was surprised to see the drawings were of *her*: one of her in the ocean, another of her dangling from the claw of the enormous crane, and a third of her sleeping in a bundle of covers on Hector's bed on the ferry from Crete. She stared at the images with a mixture of awe and embarrassment.

"I can't get that night out of my mind," Hector said from behind her.

She turned to see him in nothing but a pair of jeans. Water dripped from his wet hair down his face and chest.

"It was the best night of my life," he added.

Gertie stared back at him, speechless.

"If Nikita hadn't been interested in me, do you think things might have turned out differently between us?" he asked.

"I don't know." She turned away from him, back to the drawings on the desk. "These are amazing. You're really talented."

"Thanks." He moved closer to her and put the drawings away in a drawer.

"You don't have to put them away," she said. "I like them."

He hesitated, and then took them out again. "All right. I thought maybe…"

"What?"

"They'd make you feel uncomfortable."

Her heart was beating fast. "That was an incredible night for me, too."

He glanced at her mouth. "Really?"

She nodded.

He put a hand on her shoulder, and just when she thought he might kiss her, he asked, "What are you doing up so early, anyway? Don't you usually sleep until noon, like a normal teenager?"

She snapped out of her reverie. "I'm going to school. What do you mean?"

"You can't. Mr. and Mrs. Angelis are going to withdraw you today. I heard them talking about it."

Gertie's mouth dropped open. "Oh, no. Have they done it yet?"

He shrugged. "Even if they haven't, if you go to school, don't you think they'll find out?"

"No. Not if no one says anything."

He went to his dresser and took out a t-shirt. As he pulled it on over his head, he said, "I think you should hide out here, just in case. I'll let you know later today if Miss Piper called your name."

Miss Piper was their photography teacher.

"What about your mom?"

"She's already gone again, but she's off tonight, so I'll probably eat dinner with her and then sneak you up the leftovers."

"Okay."

"You can eat whatever you find downstairs. My mom left a pan of biscuits on the stovetop."

"Sounds good."

"And there's lots of other food in the fridge for lunch. Help yourself, okay?"

She nodded. "Thanks."

She followed him downstairs and walked him to the door, where he stopped and turned to her. "You going to be okay here, by yourself?"

She nodded again.

He leaned close and kissed her on the cheek. "Try to not to worry. We'll get everything worked out, okay? Give Mamá and Babá a chance to recover, and then you can explain everything to them."

"Okay." She smiled but on the inside she felt a lot less confident.

After he left, she sat on the big, cushy sofa in the middle of the great room and gazed up at the painting of the giant crane. For the first time in her life, she hated missing school.

For the first time in her life, she had friends and a family who cared.

How could she have lost it all in one stupid night? If only she hadn't tried to read Phoebe's mind. It wasn't Gertie's job to solve everyone's problems. If she'd minded her own business, she would still be at the Angelis apartment, where she belonged.

"What am I going to do?" she asked the portrait.

As if the bird had answered her, an idea came to her mind, swift and clear. She ran upstairs and opened her bedroom window, so she'd have a way back in at night.

Chapter Twenty-Six: Fourth Bite

The walk to the nearest bus stop from Hector's house was twenty minutes; from there, Gertie took the bus to the metro-rail and rode for twenty more minutes to the acropolis. Once there, she strolled around with the tourists, lunched at a café, and then hung out at the Parthenon all afternoon, waiting. She bought two gifts at a shop—one for Jeno and another for Hector. For Jeno, she found a soft black pillow with white letters that said, "I'm dreaming of you" on one side and "I'm thinking of you" on the other. For Hector, she bought a sketch pad and a set of charcoal pencils.

When it was time for school to end, she texted Hector and told him she would be back that evening.

"Where are you?" he texted back.

"Taking care of something, No questions."

"Need help?" he texted back.

"No."

"Let me know if you need a lift," he wrote.

"Thanks."

"Be careful," he wrote again.

Getting bored, she wished she'd brought her e-reader and then realized she could read on her phone. She had a hard time finding where she had last left off in *The Vampire Chronicles*, but once she found her place, it didn't take long for the story to suck her back in.

Before she knew it, dusk had come, and the tourists were leaving.

She slipped her arm through the handle on her shopping bag and climbed down the rock toward the caves.

I'm here to see you, Jeno, she thought as she descended.

She peered down over the ledge and saw him and his sister, along with a few others, leaving the caves and scattering in different directions. Jeno climbed the rock toward her.

When he was just a few feet away, her smile widened. Each time she saw him, he seemed more beautiful than the last. Her heart ached for him now. She wanted very much to be in his arms.

Since he could read her thoughts, he obliged her when he caught up to her by circling his arms around her waist. She reached up and kissed him.

He smiled against her lips. "You have a way of brightening my mood."

"I got you a present." She reached into her shopping bag and brought out the pillow. "When you know I'm awake, put the pillow on this side, because I'm always thinking of you when I'm awake. And when you know I'm asleep, put it on this side."

He looked at her—long and hard.

"What's wrong?" she asked.

"No one has ever given me a present before."

"Never?"

"Not since I was a little boy."

Gertie thought of the woman he had loved for thirty years.

"Not even her. Not because she didn't try."

"What do you mean?"

"She would ask me if I wanted this thing or that thing, but I always said no. I don't need clothes, because temperature doesn't bother me. I don't need hats, gloves, ties, shoes, or any of those fashionable accessories."

"Because you can make illusions."

"I'm hard to buy for. I don't like cologne."

"Why not?"

"It overwhelms my senses."

"Well, I know you don't sleep as often as I do, but when you do lie down, maybe this pillow will help you think of me." She gave him a playful wink.

He kissed the top of her head. "Indeed, though I don't need help for that."

"What about books, or art supplies?"

"I'm not much of an artist, but I do love to read."

"Then I know what to give you next." She wondered why the woman he loved had never given him books.

"Because that's what we did together. That's one of the reasons I fell in love with her."

"You read together?"

"She had a very large collection of books, and I used to stay there in her house and read to my heart's content. I lived with her for many years. I only returned to Athens the night I met you on the bus."

"I wish *we* could move in together," Gertie said.

"If we had the money for rent, we could." He smoothed her hair from her eyes and gave her another kiss on her forehead.

She tried to hide her thoughts from him, but she didn't know how.

"That's true, koureetsi mou," he said. "You would likely have to choose between me and the Angelis family."

"Well, they kicked me out, so..." she didn't finish her thought.

"But you came to me today hoping for a way to remedy that."

She really wished he couldn't read her mind.

"I'm sorry. I can't stop myself," he said.

"If I could make them forget what happened that night between me and Phoebe, then maybe I could move back in and go back to school." *And live a normal life.*

"Or you could leave them altogether and live with me," he said. "Who needs a normal life?"

"We wouldn't have rent money for long. My parents would cut me off if they found out I was living with a boy." *Not to mention a vampire.*

"We won't know until we try," he argued. "And you could always get a job."

That can be my backup plan.

"I don't like being the backup plan," Jeno murmured.

"You are a part of *both* plans. I'm not going to stop seeing you if I move back in with them." If she erased Mamá's memory, Gertie's promise to never see Jeno again would no longer be a problem.

He looked at her uncertainly.

"Besides, I won't be able to get much of a job if I don't finish high school first," she added.

"I agree." He pulled her close and rested his chin on the top of her head. "You should finish school."

She leaned her cheek against his chest. *Will you help me with my plan tonight?*

"Of course. There was never a question about that," he said. "But your plan will only work if you can get each one of them to look into your eyes."

"I'm pretty sure I can do that."

"Even though they think you've already gone back to America?"

"Nikita and Klaus know the truth."

"Good. Go to them first, and then you can manipulate them into inviting you inside. You cannot enter their apartment without an invitation now that you've been told to leave."

"Thanks for not lecturing me about using your powers to solve my problems."

"The pleasure is all mine." He closed his eyes and sighed.

She smiled up at him, taking in his beauty and thinking that one day she really would like to live with him. Maybe after high school, she would go to college in Athens, and they could be together then.

"We have many universities here to choose from." Jeno cupped her face in his hands. "What will you do after that?"

"Maybe get a job as a librarian somewhere."

"You could work the night shift and sneak me in. We could read the nights away."

"That sounds incredible."

"You really want to stay in Greece? You would renounce your parents' fortune?"

"Absolutely. This is my home now. Right here, with you."

He kissed the tip of her nose, which caused a smile to split her face in half.

"You're so cute when you smile," he said.

"But not when I don't?" She frowned.

He laughed at her. "You're even cuter when you frown."

She laughed, too, and then became aware of the drop in temperature as the darkness of the night enfolded them.

"You need to learn to dress in layers," Jeno said. "You're always so cold at night, and I can do little to help you."

"Just hold me for a while. Okay?"

"I have no problem with that."

She wondered if Hector was worried about her, since she hadn't told him where she was or when she'd be home. She wondered if she should text him.

"I think you should," Jeno said. "I can sense his anxiety."

"You're such a thoughtful person." She took out her phone and texted, "I'm safe and will be at your place later tonight."

Hector immediately texted back, "Are you with Jeno?"

"Yes," she replied. Then she turned off her phone.

"Being able to read minds is not always a benefit, you know," Jeno said.

"I know."

"It's hard to hear him thinking about you, and even worse to hear you thinking about him."

"It's *you* I love, Jeno," she gazed into his eyes. "If I had your powers I would force you to believe that."

"Kiss me instead." He touched his mouth to hers.

She closed her eyes and sank against him, her entire body delighting in the feel of his touch.

Are you ready? she wondered. *Are you ready to drink my blood?*

"I'm always ready for you, my love," Jeno whispered.

He kissed down her neck, where her pulse throbbed with anticipation. A moan fled from his throat as he broke through skin and drank.

Chapter Twenty-Seven: The Angelis Family

Gertie and Jeno flew across the city holding hands. She'd never felt so happy, or so hopeful, as she did in that moment, giggling with pleasure at the feel of the wind beneath her arms and against her face. The city lights below were stunning, and the nearly full moon in the sky above had never seemed closer, almost within reach. She surged with power, with a sense of invincibility, and wished she could always feel this way, enormously endowed with strength.

Jeno, able to read her mind, threw back his head and laughed. He agreed that this was a happy moment. His thoughts revealed his equal pleasure with her by his side. Before reaching the Angelis apartment, he turned on his back and positioned himself below her, so he could gaze up at her as they flew. She laughed again, wrapped her arms around him, and pushed them into a continuous spin. She felt dizzy and delirious with power and hope and happiness.

"I love you, Jeno!" she cried out into the night, even though his face was near hers. "I love you so much!"

He pulled her close, firm against him. "Let me have another taste of you."

She laughed again and lifted her chin to expose her neck. He sucked at her neck where he had previously marked her, and the wonderful dizziness came over her again.

"Oh, my!" She leaned against him and allowed him to navigate them through the sky as she caught her bearings.

"Oh my, indeed." He was breathless as his vampire heart pumped her blood through his veins.

Too soon, he stopped. Gertie lifted her face from Jeno's chest to find them hovering above the Angelis's apartment building.

"Are you sure you want to do this?" Jeno asked. "It may not go the way you hope."

"I have to try to win them back," she said. "I never realized what I was missing before I became a part of their family."

Jeno frowned, and she could see his memories of his own family, before they were ripped apart. His mother and father and sister had been close. He was happy then. "It was a good life," he said out loud. "I understand why this is important to you."

Gertie's eyes filled with tears of sorrow for Jeno's loss. She supposed hundreds of centuries could never take away that pain.

"Maybe I can be your family," she whispered, stroking his cheeks. "Maybe we can build a family together."

Vampires cannot reproduce.

"That's not what I mean," she said. "I mean you and me, and true friends who love us. Maybe I can help Mamá and Babá to accept you. Maybe Klaus and Nikita can grow to love you."

"I don't know."

"It starts tonight," she said. "I'm going to go to them, have them look into my eyes, and I'm going to erase their memories of the other night."

"Okay, koureetsi mou."

"Then, I'm going to suggest to them that they need to give you a chance to prove how good you are. Because you *are* good, Jeno."

It was Jeno's turn to spring tears, but he closed his eyes and held them back. As he did so, he pressed his mouth hard against hers and kissed her passionately, his mind sending out thoughts of love, hope, tenderness, and need.

"I love you," he said. "You are sweet and kind. I'm glad I didn't give up on love."

"Me, too."

He kissed the top of her head. "Are you ready, then?"

"Ready as I'll ever be. What time is it?"

Jeno glanced at the moon. "Eight o'clock, or thereabout."

She squeezed his hands, kissed him once more, and then flew down to the sidewalk in front of her building.

I'll be waiting for you right here, Jeno said to her telepathically.

Okay.

A man stared at her where she landed on the sidewalk, and she locked on his eyes and said, "You are imaging things. Get home and go to sleep."

The man smiled and said, "Good night" to her in Greek.

"Kaliníhta," she said in reply.

As she entered the building and climbed the steps toward the apartment, she reached out to Nikita.

Please come out to the stairs, Gertie said in Nikita's mind. *I need your help.*

Is that you, Gertie? Nikita wondered.

Yes, it's me. Gertie waited on the bottom of the last flight of stairs.

You're possessed?

One of the neighbors opened her door and looked at Gertie, first with curiosity, and then with horror. Gertie clapped her hand to the mark on her throat.

"Tramp stamp!" the woman cried, as she closed the door behind her.

Gertie?

Not possessed. Bitten. Please come out. Please. This is important.

Moments later, the front door to the Angelis apartment opened, and Nikita stood in the hallway. She glanced around before meeting Gertie's gaze down on the second landing.

"Invite me inside," Gertie said, using her magnetic powers. "Ask me to come in to see your family."

Nikita said, "Do you…" but before she could finish, Mamá appeared in the doorway asking, "What is this?"

Gertie attempted to cover her mark, but was too late. Mamá's eyes widened with fear and rage.

"What have you done to yourself?" she cried. "Why have you so blatantly disobeyed my wishes? I don't believe it! I don't believe you could do this to me, Gertoula!"

"Mamá, please listen!" Gertie rushed up the steps. "Look into my eyes and listen."

Mamá refused to meet Gertie's gaze. "I will not let you trick me like that. I know the ways of the tramps. I thought you cared more for me than this!" Tears spilled down Mamá's face.

Babá was soon behind her with a look of shock. "Gertie? No, it can't be true. Again?"

"Please, Babá! Please listen to me."

"Don't look at her," Mamá warned. "She's come to deceive us."

"No!" Gertie said, unable to stop the sobs from racking her body. "Please hear what I have to say. Can I come inside? I just want to talk to you. Look into my eyes."

How could she manipulate their minds if they didn't look at her? Nothing was going her way.

Klaus then appeared in the doorway. "Gertie?"

"Don't look at her," Mamá warned again.

Babá pointed his finger at her. "You have devastated this family beyond repair."

"Gertie, how could you?" Klaus gave her a look of revulsion.

"Please let me explain," Gertie begged. "Tell them how I was only trying to help, Klaus. Please, look at me!"

"No more lies!" Mamá screeched.

Two neighbors from across the hall opened their doors to stare at the scene.

"Now leave," Babá demanded of Gertie, ignoring the neighbors. "Your blatant lack of respect for us after what we have done for you is atrocious and heartbreaking. We loved you as our own daughter, and you come here like this?"

"He's right," Mamá said, sobbing as hard as Gertie was. "You must leave. We can do no more for you now. We've lost you to the tramps of the night."

"You haven't lost me," Gertie said, rushing to Mamá. "Please look at me. I love you, Mamá. You are more my mother than that woman in New York. Please don't turn away from me!"

"You mean to manipulate me?" Mamá accused. "Why?"

"I speak the truth," Gertie took Mamá's hands and pulled her close, trying to embrace her. "Please, Mamá. I love you. I need you."

Tears poured down Marta's red and quivering cheeks. Through thick sobs, she said, "I told you to have nothing to do with that vamp, and you cared nothing for my wishes. Is that love?"

Mamá ripped her arms away from Gertie and stepped back, avoiding her eyes.

Gertie turned to Babá, but he, too, lowered his eyes, his face a mixture of rage and sadness.

"Klaus, please," Gertie murmured, losing her nerve.

Klaus turned away and went back inside.

Gertie turned to her best friend in the whole wide world. "Nikita?"

Mamá put an arm around Nikita, who'd been watching the scene unfold in silent shock and misery. Gertie could read the mixed feelings in all of their minds. At least the powers of the vampire gave her that ability to see how much they did love her. But they also gave her the power to see how terribly hurt, disappointed, and outraged they were by her deeds.

Their thoughts told her that they were frightened of her and of what she might do to their family. They turned their backs on her and left her alone in the hallway.

As she turned to leave, she saw Hector standing at the bottom of the stairs looking up at her with horror. She read his thoughts of disbelief and, worse, of betrayal. He couldn't believe she would turn her back on him, especially after he had helped her.

"I'm so sorry," she said.

His eyes were moist and his face pale. "You can't stay with me and be with him. You have to choose."

She bit her quivering lip, tormented by the thought of losing another friend. There was no one left for her but Jeno. He was her one true friend who would stay with her and help her, no matter what the cost. Without looking again at Hector, she flew through a second-story window, away from the building and up into Jeno's arms.

"Take me away from here," she said, as she broke into another round of tears.

He held her close, comforting her with kisses, as he guided her across the sky back to the acropolis, to the spot where they had left her shopping bag filled with Jeno's pillow and Hector's art supplies.

She took the pad and pencils and was about to fling them over the city when Jeno stopped her.

"You can still give them to him," he said. "I'm not your only friend."

She threw herself against him. "You're so kind and good. It's just not fair that they won't accept you," she faltered, "or me."

"Lord Hades once told me that life isn't fair, but death is. When I asked him what about the undead, he had nothing to say."

"What will I do now?" Gertie asked, still sobbing uncontrollably. "Where will I go?"

Jeno smoothed her hair from her eyes and wiped her tears from her cheeks. "You still have your credit card, no?"

She nodded.

"I know of a place, a hotel that is friendly toward my kind."

"Can you stay there with me?" she asked, not wanting to be alone.

"Of course."

"My things are at Hector's house."

"They are just things. Leave them."

"I left a window open."

"But he told you to choose," he rubbed his nose against hers, "and you chose me."

"So?"

"This means you are no longer invited into his home. As long as the vampire virus runs through your blood…"

"I see." She sniffled. Except for Jeno, she had no one and nothing.

"That isn't true. You can always ask Hector for your things. He would give them to you."

"You didn't see his face."

Jeno did not reply.

Chapter Twenty-Eight: Hotel Frangelico

The Hotel Frangelico was on the darkest corner of the darkest street between the acropolis and the Omonoia Square. Gothic columns and stained glass windows with sharp angles adorned the façade. If she hadn't known better, Gertie would have thought Jeno had taken her to an old church.

Inside, the lobby was all reds, golds, and dark mahogany wood, with crystal chandeliers that gave off little light. Gertie suspected the hotel was once very fine, a hundred years ago.

She produced her credit card, and after it was approved, had no trouble securing a room for the two of them.

"One bed or two?" the old woman behind the counter asked, in Greek, in a thick Mediterranean accent.

Gertie glanced over at Jeno. "Um…"

"Dhyo," Jeno said, which meant "two."

"How many nights?" the woman asked.

"Three," Gertie said.

And what if your mission takes longer and your parents cancel the card? Jeno asked telepathically.

"Actually, I'd like to pre-pay for an entire week," Gertie said.

The old woman said nothing about their lack of luggage as she handed over the key, but Gertie could read her mind. She considered Jeno a tramp and Gertie an addict, and the woman didn't care, because her business was founded on such relationships. Tramps preyed on rich victims, who were more than happy to pay for a nice hotel stay in exchange for their fix. The hotel welcomed these customers, until they ran out of money.

The couple in line behind them smiled courteously as Gertie and Jeno walked past. Gertie noticed a tramp stamp on the man's throat and caught a brief view of fangs in the woman's mouth. As she and Jeno continued toward the elevators, they passed a bar. Gertie stopped to gawk.

The tramps were openly vampires here, especially in the bar, where music played, and sexy bartenders danced on tables. The vampires sat and talked and laughed with their fangs bared, and the humans did not balk. Instead, the humans appeared stoned out of their minds, in a permanent stupor that rendered them helpless. And it was nearly four in the morning.

"Why did you bring me here?" she whispered.

He guided her onto the elevator. "Because it's safe."

Safe for vampires, she thought, *but maybe not for humans*.

"For humans, too," he said as the elevator doors closed. "Trust me."

That's when she noticed the mirrors on the elevator walls. She nearly jumped from her shoes because it was eerily jarring not to see their reflections looking back at them. She inspected her arms and legs, double-checking that she was still visible, which she was. Then she stared in awe at the missing reflections in the mirror.

"Our cells reflect light, but that light cannot be reflected a second time," Jeno explained. "It dies in the air around us."

"That's so bizarre," she said, studying the mirror. "I should have expected this." The same was true in all the vampire lore she had ever read.

"I've not been able to see my reflection in a body of water or a piece of glass for centuries, and yet it still unsettles me."

A hazy, transparent outline of Gertie appeared in the mirror before they reached their floor.

"The vampire virus is fading from your body." He took her hand and kissed it.

She watched with fascination at her shimmering reflection beside his missing one.

When they reached the seventh floor, they were met by another couple waiting to board the elevator.

A girl, who looked about Gertie's age, gave them a smile full of fangs. "Going down?" she asked in Greek.

The boy beside her wore a tramp stamp on his neck and a grin on his face. "Watch this!" He disappeared, only to reappear in the elevator. "Cool, huh?"

His clothes must be an illusion, she realized. Gertie saw a bit of herself in his fascination. She could see how Jeno and other vampires would grow weary of the attitude of their human prey. It was always a novelty to someone, she supposed.

"It's not a bad life," the girl vampire said.

Was she responding to Gertie's thoughts?

"Do yourself a favor and don't think so hard and so deeply," the girl vampire said to Gertie. "Life is what it is. Just enjoy it, dearie."

"This is our stop." Jeno held the elevator doors for Gertie as she stepped out into the hallway.

"Thanks," Gertie said to the other vampire.

"Good night," the vampire replied as the doors closed between them.

Jeno led her down the dark hallway. The red and gold carpeting was full of stains, and the crème-colored paint on the walls was chipped along the baseboards and corners.

This hotel needs some serious updating, she thought.

"At least you'll be safe here," Jeno said, stopping before their room.

He took the key and opened the door to what she supposed was her new home—at least temporarily. The color scheme from the lobby and hallways continued in this three-room suite with its sitting room, bathroom, and bedroom. A sliding glass door opened from the bedroom onto a balcony that faced the acropolis—its bright lights shining prominently above the city.

Gertie and Jeno stood together on the balcony, holding hands.

"I'm scared, Jeno."

He pulled her into his arms. "I will take good care of you."

"What if Mamá and Babá never forgive me? What if Nikita and Klaus and Phoebe and Hector never want to speak to me again?"

He stroked her hair and gazed down at her with a smile. "That will never happen. Can you not hear their thoughts?"

She closed her eyes and focused on Nikita, but heard nothing.

"The virus must be leaving your body," Jeno said. "But I can hear them. They are all hurt and confused and frightened, but they have not stopped caring for you, koureetsi mou."

"Oh, Jeno," she threw her arms around his neck. "Please bite me again, so I can hear their thoughts."

"But it's nearly morning. You won't be able to tolerate the sunlight with the virus pumping through your veins."

New tears poured down her cheeks. "Oh, please? I'm so depressed and worried. You and I can spend the day inside the room. I don't need to be out in the daylight."

He kissed her wet cheeks, wiping her tears with his lips. She ran her fingers through his thick, curly hair. The fatigue that always set in after the vampire powers had faded from her body was beginning to overtake her.

"Please, Jeno," she whispered. "Take my blood once more. Just enough to help me hear their thoughts."

His eyebrows bent together. "I'll have to make a new mark. The one on your neck has already begun to heal."

"That's okay. I don't mind. Oh, please." She could sense his arousal, as his hands trembled and his mouth sought hers.

"I fear we are becoming what we both wished not to be," he whispered breathlessly, as he moved his lips to her neck.

"What do you mean?" she asked with her eyes closed and her heart desperate.

He lifted her wrist to his mouth and sank his fangs in hard.

She gasped and opened her eyes wide as he sucked eagerly. The room began to spin, but despite the euphoria gently sweeping through her system, she was frightened. Just before she was about to say something, he stopped.

"I'm sorry." He wrapped his long fingers around her wrist and applied pressure to the bite.

Blood continued to drip down her arm as he squeezed. He licked it up as though he were holding a melting ice cream cone. For the first time since she had been with him, she shuddered at the sight.

Jeno frowned. "I'm sorry. I got carried away. It will never happen again."

As soon as the spinning stopped, Gertie sought Nikita's presence, looking first in their room. She found her and read her thoughts:

If only she would leave him, she could go back to the person she was. She could be my best friend, my sister. Why did she have to change? And will she ever go back to being my Gertie? The real Gertie? And not this possessed monster that has hurt my family?

Gertie broke away from Nikita, unable to listen anymore.

"She wants you to leave me," Jeno said, having read her thoughts. "She might be right."

"Don't say that." Gertie squeezed his shoulders and looked deeply into his eyes. "Please believe me when I say I love you."

He gave her a tender smile. "You can't use mind control on me, but that was a nice try."

"I'm serious."

"I know." He kissed her.

Although she was terrified of what she would hear, Gertie sought out Mamá. Her thoughts were in Greek, but the vampire virus made their meaning clear:

Yes, I will have to call Danielle in the morning, when it is evening there. The only thing to do is for her to come and rescue her daughter. I'm such a failure. I should have known better than to bring another child into this home.

249

Tears tumbled down Gertie's cheeks.

"Please don't cry, koureetsi mou," Jeno said, swiping her tears with his thumbs.

"Mamá thinks it's her fault. That she's a failure."

"Come and sit with me."

They went inside and closed the balcony door. Jeno drew the curtains and then led Gertie back to the sitting room. Side by side they sat on the sofa. Jeno put his feet up on the coffee table and held her in his arms. She laid her head on his lap and curled her legs over the opposite arm of the sofa.

She read his thoughts. He was upset with himself for taking so much of her blood. He needed to use more restraint and to think of her before his own needs. He wished he never would have tasted her blood. Neither of them would be in this mess if he had stuck to his original intentions.

"Stop, Jeno. You did this for *me*."

"I wish that were true, my love." He stroked her hair.

Gertie now sought out Klaus. She knew her reactions to Hector's thoughts would only hurt Jeno, so she avoided them, but this small bit came through: *I didn't mean what I said. You can be with him and stay with me. I didn't mean it.*

She fought the urge to continue in his mind.

When she focused on Klaus, she found him weeping. *My poor little brother and sister. If Mamá and Babá will do nothing, I must do something. Damien must be put out of his misery. A wooden stake through his heart. It's the only way. And while I'm at it, the other vampire should be put out of his as well. Then maybe Gertie will be free of her addiction.*

Gertie flinched and looked up at Jeno. "Klaus wants to drive a stake through Damien's heart."

"And my father's," Jeno said. "That would destroy hundreds of vampires."

A few moments later, the hotel door burst open, and a half a dozen vampires stood in the entry with seething looks on their faces. They were a mixed group of young and old and male and female. Two were tall and lanky, one was as muscular as a boxer, two wore their hair in colorful spikes, and another, an older woman, was small but the scariest of them all.

"What did you just say, Jeno?" the older woman hissed.

Go from here now, Gertie! Jeno screamed in Gertie's head. *Go to Hector.*

"But, Jeno!"

"Go!"

As she scrambled from the sofa, one of the intruding vampires, the muscular one, dashed toward her, but Jeno sprang at him. One of the spikey-haired vampires swooped across the room. Jeno grabbed the floor lamp and swung it like a baseball bat, knocking the vampire into the wall. Terrified for her life, Gertie ran to the balcony and jumped into the predawn sky, flying as fast as she could toward Hector's house.

She sailed over the city, her heart pounding in her chest.

What's going on, Jeno? she asked. *Are you okay?*

Don't worry about me. They're coming after you.

Why?

At that moment, she spotted one of the vampires closing in on her—the old woman. Gertie picked up speed in a nose dive directly down toward Hector's subdivision.

Before she reached his house, she felt a grip on her ankle. It was one of the tall and lanky males, and he looked fierce. She kicked and flailed through the air, but she could not lose her attacker. Then the other tall and lanky vampire joined the first, and she was trapped in their cold arms.

"The sun is rising," one said to another.

"To the caves!"

Chapter Twenty-Nine: The Labyrinth

The two vampires raced across the Adriatic Sea and plummeted down toward Crete with Gertie in their clutches. Gertie closed her eyes and screamed when it looked like they were going to crash into the hillside. Although she bumped against something hard, she did not crash.

"You got it?" one vamp said to the other near the mouth of a cave.

"Yes. Go!"

They wound through the tunneling caverns with Gertie in between them, and then, like a bomber dropping its cargo, they let her fall before they turned back.

The vampire virus was still in her body, because she could see even though very little light showed through the cracks in the rock eight feet above her. The tunnel was narrow and wet. The ground was cold and covered in small pebbles, which moved like sand beneath her hands as she pushed herself into a sitting position.

She caught her breath and then sought Jeno by focusing on the Hotel Frangelico. When she found him, she entered his mind to ask what was going on. *Why did they do this?*

It's because of Klaus's plan. They overheard us talking about it.

So why did they abduct me?

Leverage.

Huh?

They believe the Angelis family will turn over my father in exchange for you.

She let that sink in. She wasn't so sure Mamá and Babá and Klaus would make that trade.

Of course they would, Jeno said in her mind.

Where am I? She climbed to her feet and dusted off the back of her jeans.

The island of Crete, beneath the palace ruins in Knossos, in the caves known as the labyrinth.

And what about you? Are you okay?

They left me here in our room. They know I can't leave while the sun is out.

I'm glad you're safe. She wiped her eyes with the back of her hand.

I'm so sorry, koureetsi mou. I thought you would be safe here, too.

So they freaked out because they heard us mention Klaus's thoughts? We don't even know if he was serious.

The destruction of my father would mean their own—at least for many of them. They take these things quite seriously.

What are we going to do?

I'll come for you as soon as night falls.

What about the Angelis family? Are they safe? She began to follow the tunnel to see where it would lead.

At least until nightfall. After that, I'm not so sure.

Her knees trembled and almost gave out with her realization that her host family would soon be in danger. "This is all my fault."

Do not speak out loud! And stay where you are! Jeno's voice commanded, pounding in her head.

She froze. *Jeno? What are you not telling me?*

People go mad trying to escape the labyrinth. Just stay where you are until I can come for you. Your abductors used string to find their way back out; I'll do the same.

She glanced in front and behind her, sensing a presence. *And I shouldn't speak because...*

You'll awaken the Minotaur.

Gertie heard something coming toward her around the bend behind her. *I think it's too late.*

An earth-quaking roar, along with the sound of heavy footsteps, confirmed her suspicions. She took off running through the winding tunnel in the opposite direction. Her vampire powers gave her incredible speed, but the sharp turns of the tunnel slowed her down, and soon the Minotaur was at her heels.

Panting, she glanced back to see his angry bull head growling at her and his muscular man's arms reaching out for her. Barely escaping his grasp, she followed the tunnel around another bend and scraped her shoulder on a rock jutting out from the wall. It stung and brought tears to her eyes, but she kept going, round and round the bends, without any end in sight.

Sight.

Maybe she could use invisibility to hide from the beast. Without stopping, she pulled her energy into her core, imagining herself a turtle pulling into its shell. After a few moments, she could no longer see her hands, but her entire body was still visible in her clothes—longs sleeves, jeans, boots. As fast as she could, she tugged off her shirt and threw it into the Minotaur's face. It blinded him for only a second as he whipped it off his head, leaving her no time to remove her other clothing.

As she turned around another bend, the Minotaur grabbed her leg, causing her to tumble to her hands and knees. She spun around on her back and used her free leg and vampire strength to kick the monster's snout. He wailed with pain and released her. She scrambled off the ground and flew up to the highest point of the cave. Still within reach of the Minotaur, she kicked off her boots, aiming for his head. They hit their mark, and the Minotaur groaned.

"Why, you…" He threw her boots across the tunnel.

Her vampire strength and speed gave her a fighting chance. She slipped off the rest of her clothing and flew away.

Near the top of the cavern several yards from the Minotaur, Gertie, invisible, stopped to catch her breath, but as soon as she exhaled, the monster charged toward her again. She flew along the ceiling of the caverns until she ran into a colony of bats. Their wings beat against her as they rushed away from her. One got tangled in her hair, and she shrieked and flapped her hands.

The Minotaur caught up to her and swung his arms in her direction. When his hand hit her knee, she screamed again and darted past him. Then she flew too fast around a corner and bashed her head into a stalactite. She fell to the floor, dazed. Even worse, she was visible and, to her mortification, naked.

Covering herself with her hands as best she could, she closed her eyes and waited for the Minotaur to kill her. She listened to his thoughts:

...new vampires think they can come in here...let her fall into a coma then, and I'll drag her body out like I've done others stupid enough to enter without their thread.

When the strike never came, she opened her eyes to see the beast glaring down at her.

"What are you waiting for?" she asked angrily.

"Do you have a death wish?" he asked her.

"Not really," she said, confused by the question. "Does it matter?"

"Do you know how many vampires have attempted to deceive me? They sit in here like spiders, waiting for the mortals to come and get lost—which happens on a regular basis. How many mortals have died here to you blood-suckers? And when they fail to return home to their loved ones, who gets blamed?"

From the neck down, he looked like a normal man—large and muscular, but nevertheless, a man, in black cargo pants, boots, and a thin shirt. Only his head resembled a bull.

"What are you talking about? I'm not a vampire."

He took a step closer. "You look like one."

"Why do you care what I am?"

"Why are you here?" he demanded.

"Two vampires kidnapped me and left me here."

He turned his back to her and stormed off.

She pulled her energy inward as hard as she could, but the pain in her head and her overall exhaustion made it too hard to focus. Invisibility no longer was an option, and this was pretty inconvenient since she was without her clothes.

Just as she was contemplating whether she should go back for her clothes or try to escape without them, they were hurled at her from the returning beast.

He brought her clothes back?

"Get dressed," he said, tossing her wallet and phone, which must have fallen from her back pockets, in her direction. "And then tell me why you're here."

He turned away from her as she slipped on her clothes and boots. The whole time, she wondered why he hadn't killed her. His thoughts gave nothing away, only indicating that he felt wary of the vampires and their constant intrusions into his domain. Gertie was relieved to have her wallet and phone, even though the phone was dead.

"Asterion?" a woman's voice called though the cavern. "Where are you?"

"Over here," the beast replied. "We have company, so dim yourself."

A beautiful woman with auburn hair and a loose-fitting gown emerged from around the bend. "Is she a tramp?"

"I don't know yet," the monster said. "She looks like one but claims to be human."

"I *am* human," Gertie insisted. "I've been bitten, but I haven't been turned."

The Minotaur spoke in a nicer tone to the woman. "She claims a couple of vampires abandoned her here."

"They are using me as leverage." Gertie climbed to her feet, clinging to the cavern walls for balance. Her head was killing her.

"For what?" the young woman asked.

Gertie told them about Damien and Jeno's father and Klaus's thoughts.

"I would love to see the father of the vampires destroyed," the Minotaur said when Gertie had finished. "There are too many of them. They have to stoop to drastic measures to survive."

"Why does that concern the Minotaur?" Gertie asked.

"Please don't call him that," the woman scolded. "His proper name is Asterion."

"Oh. Sorry."

"And I'm Ariadne," the woman added.

Gertie couldn't believe it. She knew a bit about the nymph's history. Ariadne once helped Theseus to slay the Minotaur, even though the beast was her half bother.

"I live here with my brother and do my best to protect him from being mistreated."

"But I thought..." Gertie stopped short. The myths weren't always accurate. Maybe Theseus hadn't slayed her brother.

"The rumors about him aren't true," Ariadne continued. "He doesn't eat mortals. People with something to prove come into the labyrinth all the time. They see it as a challenge. They come without their string. The vampires lay in wait. The mortals are killed and everyone blames Asterion."

"Well, I'm not a vampire," Gertie said. "As soon as the virus fades from my system, you'll see I'm telling the truth."

The Minotaur crossed his arms at his chest. "If the blood-suckers plan to retrieve their father's tomb from the mortals, then that means..."

"The uprising," Ariadne finished.

"Uprising?" Gertie asked.

"Dionysus has spoken of it for centuries," Ariadne said.

"But he feared the mortals would retaliate by driving a stake through their father's heart," Asterion added. "That would wipe out several hundred, maybe thousands, of them."

Ariadne tapped her lower lip with an index finger. "If the vampires trade you for their father, then…"

"There would be nothing holding Dionysus back," Gertie finished.

She had to warn the others. She sought out Hector, but couldn't find him.

Jeno, we have to warn them. Where's Hector?

The vampire did not reply.

Chapter Thirty: Awakenings

Ariadne and Asterion guided Gertie to the mouth of the labyrinth, but Gertie, trying in vain to contact Hector and Jeno, continued to hide in the dark until after the vampire virus wore off and she could tolerate sunlight again. The siblings were remarkably friendly to her, once she was fully human. They shared their stories with her to help with the passing of time. Ariadne told her about the time she had helped Theseus. Apparently the two were supposed to be married, but the hero moved on without her. When Asterion had returned from the Underworld after being slayed by Theseus, Ariadne vowed to make it up to her brother. The nymph had remained by Asterion's side ever since. Occasionally, Dionysus came around asking for her hand in marriage, but, because of her vow to her brother, Ariadne turned the god of wine away. Asterion said that his job now was to protect humans from getting lost in the labyrinth.

"I thought Daedalus created this maze to keep you prisoner?" Gertie asked.

"Originally, he did," Asterion said. "But you can't live here for centuries and not figure out the puzzle."

"I wonder why you continue to be thought of as a monster," Gertie said—though she hadn't meant to say that out loud.

Asterion's bull head actually blushed. "I scare the hell out of them when they come, hoping they won't come back."

"He chases them back to the entrance, so they find their way," Ariadne said. "Unless the vampires get to them first."

Although Gertie was glad to be in the sunshine again, her inability to reach out to Jeno and Hector made her feel helpless. Plus, the pain in her head and the fatigue that enveloped her body made her long to be bitten again. Even worse, she was trapped on Crete, far away from her host family, and she desperately needed to warn them.

She couldn't decide whether she should wait for Jeno to come back for her at dusk, or take the ferry back to the mainland. Travelling by ferry would take at least five hours, and she wouldn't arrive much earlier than nightfall, anyway. But what if Jeno was captured? That would explain why he hadn't answered her. And, even if Jeno was safe, what if her abductors got to her before he could? Maybe she wasn't safe here in the labyrinth, even though her new friends said they would do their best to protect her. Maybe she needed to get to Hector and the Angelis family as soon as possible.

Unable to wait around doing nothing while danger was imminent, Gertie decided to take the ferry. She felt like crap and was totally exhausted. It might be nice to sleep in a bed.

Once she had boarded, she managed to borrow a phone from a fellow passenger who spoke English. She called Hector.

"Hello?"

She'd never been happier to hear his voice.

"Hector, it's Gertie. I have to tell you something important."

"Guys, it's Gertie."

"Are you with Klaus and Nikita?"

"I'm driving them home from school."

Turning away from the woman whose phone she had borrowed, Gertie quietly explained to him what had happened at the Hotel Frangelico.

"You have to warn Klaus and the others," she added. "As soon as night falls. . . Oh, Hector. I'm so sorry. This is all my fault. The vampires will be coming for Jeno's father. I'm scared of what else they might do."

"Listen to me, Gertie," Hector said. "Are you listening?"

She clenched her teeth, trying not to cry. "Uh-huh."

"Go to the hexagon in Omonoia Square and stay there until I come for you."

"But…"

"Please, Gertie!" Hector shouted angrily. "If you have any feelings for me at all, do as I say."

"But how will that help anything?" she asked.

"It will keep you safe." His voice cracked on that final word. "Get there before sundown."

"Okay," she said, though, she still wasn't completely convinced that she should. "Just please protect the others. And be careful."

She returned the phone to its owner and left the deck for her cabin, where she immediately crawled into bed. Too much was going on inside of her, though, and it got in the way of sleep. So she tried to talk to Jeno, in case he was listening. She was really worried about him, now. Maybe the other vampires had read his mind and had taken him as their prisoner, to prevent him from interfering with the vampires' plans.

Oh, Jeno. Please be okay. Please be okay!

She tossed and turned, finding that each time she was about to drift to sleep, she would seek out Jeno, hoping to hear his reply. She did this again and again, at least a dozen times over the span of two hours, nearly in tears with fatigue and worry, until, at last, at some point, she fell asleep.

A knock at her door awoke her from a terrible dream, in which every member of her host family had been murdered by vampire rebels. She must have been crying in her sleep, because her pillow and cheeks were damp.

"Time to go ashore!" a voice called from the corridor, once in Greek and again in English. Whoever it was continued down the passageway, repeating, "Time to go ashore!" and knocking on the other cabin doors.

The thirty minute bus ride into Athens felt like an eternity as she watched the sun set through her window. She hoped and prayed she would get to Omonoia Square before her abductors found her.

It was dusk when she exited the bus and started walking toward the square, hoping it was the right thing to do. Uncertainty plagued her, because she wanted to be there with Hector to help defend her host family. As she walked, she continually reached out to Jeno, but came up with nothing. When she turned the corner, though, she nearly shouted for joy. Jeno stood there, waiting for her.

She threw her arms around his neck. "Thank goodness you're all right! Why haven't you answered me?"

He put an arm around her and led her down the sidewalk. "I had to block my mind, so the others couldn't read my thoughts. Are you okay? You're not hurt? I was worried sick."

"I'm okay. I met the Minotaur."

He shook his head. "Thee moy. How did you get away?"

"It turns out he's a nice guy."

"I find that hard to believe. I know many vampires who are terrified of him."

"Maybe he was just crushing on me." She smiled and winked.

He laughed. "Now *that* I believe."

Gertie noticed they had passed the square.

"Wait. Hector wants me to wait at the square."

He stopped and cupped her cheeks. "Oh. I thought you wanted to help protect Marta's family."

She did. "I doubt I can be much help," she said. "Unless you give me your powers again."

"Just tell me what you want to do." He looked deeply into her eyes.

"I, I want to go with you." Was he using mind control on her? "I want you to drink my blood."

She could feel him trembling beneath her hands as she caressed his back.

"Are you sure you're okay?" she asked.

"Now that you're here with me again, I am. I was terrified that I might have lost you."

"Oh, Jeno." She kissed his cheeks, then his mouth.

He returned her kisses and said, against her lips, "Without you, I have no reason."

"Don't say that."

"It's true. If I hadn't met you, I wouldn't care one way or the other about the uprising. But now I have a reason to fight."

"Let's fight together," she said, squeezing his hands. "Give me the power I need to help."

"Not out in the open."

He took her hand and led her around the corner and into a dark alley. Then he pushed her against the wall of a building and kissed her madly. Her heart raced with excitement as she anticipated the power she was about to gain. She stretched her chin into the air, begging him to hurry.

"Please, oh, please. Now!"

Jeno bit into her throat and ravished her.

The euphoria came over her, along with the dizziness, though she recovered more quickly than usual. The first thing she tried to do was read Jeno's mind, but he still had it blocked.

"I have to keep *everyone* out," he said. "Shall we fly? We might not have much more time."

"Let's go."

Hand in hand, they flew up and over the city toward the Angelis apartment building.

They arrived in time to see the family around the dinner table, eating. Gertie felt nostalgic, wishing she could be among them. They seemed sad and quiet tonight. Maybe they missed her and were worried about her. She felt sort of like Ebenezer Scrooge with the ghost of Christmas Present. She wondered why they weren't up in arms after her warning. Why were they going about their evening as usual? Hadn't Hector told them that the vampires were coming?

Suddenly Mamá slapped her hand against the table. The other members of the family looked at her and froze.

"I've done as you asked," Mamá said. "I've thought about what you said, Klaus. And you, too, Nico. But I can't let you do it." She broke into tears. "I can't let you do it."

Gertie turned to read Jeno's expression and was stunned by the presence of the six vampires from the Hotel Frangelico gathered behind him. A few yards away, dozens more vampires hovered in the air, waiting. None of them had bothered to make themselves invisible. Although it was dark enough that people might not notice, to anyone studying the stars, the vampires would be a major shock.

"What's going on?" she asked Jeno through quivering lips.

"We're going to awaken my father," Jeno said. "Come on."

He took her hand and, along with the others, flew down to the apartment entrance. The front door was never locked, and the door to the basement was just off the entryway to the first floor.

The whole thing about a vampire needing to be invited inside must have been a law rather than a magical force, because Jeno and the six other vampires had no trouble entering a building where they were not welcome. The rest of them surrounded the block.

"Jeno, why are you doing this?" Gertie whispered as they flew down the basement stairs. "If your father leaves, there will be nothing in the way of the uprising."

"I don't want him destroyed," Jeno said. "He's my father."

"You heard what Dionysus said. You've heard the rumors. You're almost guaranteeing that the rebels will take over this city."

"What would be so bad about that?" he asked, when they had reached the basement floor. "We've been living in caves for

269

centuries, unwelcomed, shunned, and disadvantaged. Let the mortals change places with us for a while."

Gertie couldn't believe what she was hearing.

"Jeno, *I'm* a mortal."

"And we can change that, if you'd like."

She stood there at the base of the steps in silent shock, as the other six vampires surrounded the larger of the two coffins.

"Anyway, I don't care about the uprising so much as I want to save my father, and I'm going to need your help." Jeno took her hand and led her to the coffin. "You will help me, won't you, Gertie?"

Gertie suddenly realized what Jeno intended to do. He intended to feed his father her blood.

One by one, the vampires broke the chains around the larger coffin. When the final chain was busted, several of the wooden doors in the basement opened, and five warriors with their swords drawn charged the scene. Hector was among them.

The warriors—one woman and four men—ranged in age from eighteen to thirty-five, with Hector being the youngest. They carried swords and shields, and they were glowing, like gods.

Before Gertie could think or respond, Hector spun around like a tornado and sliced off the heads of two of the vampires. One of the heads dropped at her feet. She screamed and hid her face in Jeno's chest.

"I told you to go to the square!" Hector shouted at her.

Jeno lifted her into the air and crossed to the other side of the coffin. The other three vampires immediately positioned themselves between Jeno and the warriors as Jeno opened the tomb. Gertie barely knew what was happening when Jeno sunk his fangs into her wrist and then held it to his father's lips. The ambushing warriors beheaded two of the remaining vampires, and then Hector stabbed his blade through the chest of the third. The third had gone invisible, but when the blade met his flesh, he reappeared as he fell to the ground, dead.

Jeno held Gertie close and growled, "Back off, or I'll kill the girl."

"You wouldn't dare," Hector said through gritted teeth. "You're in love with her."

"But *I'm* not," came an ancient voice from the tomb.

Jeno's father sat up and pulled Gertie into the coffin. The dank smell made her nauseous, as she kicked and screamed and scrambled against the vampire's grasp. Her superhuman strength was nothing compared to that of the older vampire.

Hector's face turned white.

"Jeno, please!" she cried.

Hector swung his blade toward Jeno's neck, and Gertie screamed.

"No, Hector!"

She managed to pull away from the older vampire's grasp—maybe he let her go—and fly between Hector and Jeno. Hector's blade stopped about an inch away from her face.

271

The hesitation was long enough for Jeno and his father to pull her with them up the basement steps and out of the apartment building. Flanked by both vampires in the dark sky, and surrounded by dozens more, Gertie turned back to see Hector running along the street beneath her, calling out her name. Tears stung her eyes. She hadn't meant for any of this to happen.

Jeno tightened his arm around her waist. "It's going to be okay, koureetsi mou."

He kissed her hand, which was bloody still from where he'd bit her. He licked her hand and arm clean and took another taste from the open wound at her wrist.

She closed her eyes to the euphoria the virus gave her as it re-entered her blood stream and travelled to her brain. This time, however, something was different. This time, a deep, dark yearning took possession of her. As they flew down toward the acropolis, Gertie found herself in desperate need of something.

The thing she needed was human blood.

About the Author

Eva Pohler writes fiction and teaches writing and literature at a university in San Antonio, where she lives with her husband, three children, and two dogs. Eva is also the author of *The Gatekeeper's Saga, The Purgatorium Series,* and *The Mystery Book Collection.* Check her website for details at http://www.evapohler.com. You can also subscribe to her newsletter to keep up with the latest freebies and news here: http://www.evapohler.com.

If you would like to join Eva's Facebook fan club, Eva's G[R]EEKS, please request to be added here: https://www.facebook.com/groups/561869600580901/.

Acknowledgements

The completion of this book would not have been possible without the love and support of my family, especially that of my parents, husband, and children. I am also forever grateful to my street team, Eva's Divas, for all they have done to get the word out about my work.

CPSIA information can be obtained at www.ICGtesting.com
Printed in the USA
LVOW07s0056030616

491032LV00005B/169/P